**It's their last summer of being single!
Off duty, these three nurses, and
one midwife, are young, free and fabulous—
*for the moment…***

Work hard and play hard could be flatmates
Ruby, Ellie, Jess and Tilly's motto.
By day these three trainee nurses and
one newly qualified midwife are lifesavers
at Eastern Beaches hospital, but by night
they're seeking love in Sydney—
and only sexy doctors need apply!

Together they've made it through
their first year in the hospital—
full of shatteringly emotional shifts,
tough new bosses and the patching together
of broken hearts from inappropriate crushes
over a glass of wine (or two!)

Read on to meet the drop-dead gorgeous doc
who sweeps Ellie out of her scrubs.
You can also read Jess's story this month.
And, if you missed Ruby and Tilly's stories,
CORT MASON—DR DELECTABLE
by Carol Marinelli
and
SURVIVAL GUIDE TO DATING YOUR BOSS
by Fiona McArthur
are available from www.millsandboon.co.uk

Emily Forbes began her writing life as a partnership between two sisters who are both passionate bibliophiles. As a team, Emily had ten books published—and one of her proudest moments was when her tenth book was nominated for the 2010 Australian Romantic Book of the Year Award.

While Emily's love of writing remains as strong as ever, the demands of life with young families have recently made it difficult to work on stories together. But rather than give up her dream Emily now writes solo. The challenges may be different, but the reward of having a book published is still as sweet as ever.

Whether as a team or as an individual, Emily hopes to keep bringing stories to her readers. Her inspiration comes from everywhere—stories she hears while travelling, at mothers' lunches, in the media and in her other career as a physiotherapist— all get embellished with a large dose of imagination until they develop a life of their own.

If you would like to get in touch with Emily you can e-mail her at emilyforbes@internode.on.net, and she can also be found blogging at the Harlequin Medical Romance blog—www.harlequin.com

Recent titles by the same author:

NAVAL OFFICER TO FAMILY MAN
DR DROP-DEAD-GORGEOUS
THE PLAYBOY FIREFIGHTER'S PROPOSAL

Did you know these are also available as eBooks?
Visit www.millsandboon.co.uk

BREAKING HER NO-DATES RULE

BY
EMILY FORBES

First published in Great Britain 2011
by Mills & Boon, an imprint of Harlequin (UK) Limited.
Large Print edition 2012
Harlequin (UK) Limited, Eton House,
18-24 Paradise Road, Richmond, Surrey TW9 1SR

© Emily Forbes 2011

ISBN: 978 0 263 22440 5

Harlequin (UK) policy is to use papers that are
natural, renewable and recyclable products and made
from wood grown in sustainable forests. The logging
and manufacturing process conform to the legal
environmental regulations of the country of origin.

Printed and bound in Great Britain
by CPI Antony Rowe, Chippenham, Wiltshire

Dear Reader,

This is the first time I've been involved in writing a book that's part of a series with other authors and I loved every minute of it.

We came from four corners of Australia to meet in Coogee Beach, Sydney, where the stories are set, and to chat about our characters and our plans for them. Coogee is a gorgeous spot, even in the middle of winter the sun was shining and the beach was bustling, and we could picture our characters walking on the beach, meeting in the 'Stat Bar', climbing the hill to the 'hospital' and bringing their men home to 'Hill Street'.

Despite being scattered all over Australia having the 'house' in Coogee kept us together in spirit and when I picture our heroines I see the four of us as well and I imagine us in that house partying and commiserating with our characters!

We had great fun bringing these girls together and I hope you enjoy reading Ellie's story and catching up with Ruby, Tilly and Jess too.

Love,

Emily

For Sophie Grace,
one of my many gorgeous nieces.
This book will be released as you celebrate
two major milestones, your eighteenth
birthday and the end of your school days.
This is my gift to you as you enter the next
stage of your life; I hope it is everything
you've ever dreamed of. Wishing you every
success and happiness, with all my love,
Auntie K

PROLOGUE

THE old gate at 71 Hill Street squeaked in protest as Ellie shoved it open. The noise went unnoticed by her as she was intent on getting inside, getting home. Tears blurred her vision and she struggled to fit her key into the front door. She was mortified. She wanted to climb into bed, pull the covers over her head and hide from the world.

Finally the door opened and she stumbled through it. She felt physically sick and she got to the bathroom with seconds to spare before she vomited. She leant her head against the cool surface of the tiled wall as she waited to see if her stomach had emptied itself of her dinner. The rich meat she'd ordered didn't combine well with the nausea that rumbled through her following Rob's announcement. She'd been so nervous throughout dinner she'd barely tasted her meal and now she wondered why she'd bothered eating at all.

Physically she felt better once her stomach was empty, although emotionally she felt battered and bruised. She rinsed her face and brushed her teeth but the minute the toothpaste hit her stomach she felt herself start to gag again. With one hand she quickly gathered her blonde hair into a ponytail and held it out of the way as she vomited a second time.

Jess and Tilly left the hospital together after their late shifts and walked down Hill Street to number 71; home. Heading straight for the kitchen, Jess put the kettle on and searched through the bread bin for penicillin-free bread. Someone really needed to get to the shops she thought, they were living on takeaways and toast and if they didn't shop soon ther wouldn't even be any toast. She found a couple of slices of bread that looked edible and slid them into the toaster.

From the bathroom the girls could hear the sound of running water followed by vomiting.

'Is that Ruby?' Tilly asked.

Jess shrugged. 'No idea.' They'd arrived home together so she knew no more about what was going on in the house at the moment than Tilly did. And with four, and sometimes five, people sharing a house, there were plenty of things happening. Despite the colour-coded calendar in the kitchen no one could be expected to keep up to date with all the action.

Tilly went into the passage and knocked on the bathroom door. 'Ruby, is that you? Are you okay?'

'What are you doing?' Ruby's voice came from behind them, startling them both.

Tilly turned around. 'We thought you were in the bathroom. We could hear vomiting,' she explained.

Ruby came down the stairs, shaking her head. 'Not me,' she said with a shrug. 'But Adam's back. I heard him come home and he had company.'

'It could be Ellie,' Jess said hopefully. She didn't want to think of Adam's company.

'Ellie's supposed to be having dinner with Rob,' Ruby replied.

The bathroom door opened and Ellie emerged, white faced and shivering with black smudges of mascara under her eyes. Tilly, Ruby and Jess stepped back, enlarging their semi-circle to make room for her.

'What are you doing home?'

'What happened to dinner with Rob?'

'Are you sick?'

Ellie looked from one friend to the next as they each asked a question. She opened her mouth but no sound came out.

The girls could see Ellie's lips moving but there was nothing to hear. 'Something's wrong,' Ruby said to the others. She took Ellie's hand and led her through to the lounge where she sat her down. Her hands were like ice. 'Someone grab a blanket, I think she's in shock.' Had she been in an accident? Ruby searched Ellie's body for clues but there was no sign of an injury—no scratches, no blood, no bruises. 'Ellie, talk to us. What happened? Are you hurt?'

Jess returned, carrying a box of tissues and

the quilt from Ellie's bed. She draped the quilt around her shoulders. 'Was there an accident?'

Ellie shook her head. Physically she was unharmed, but how did she explain the night she'd had? None of them knew that when she'd gone out to dinner with her boyfriend of three months she'd been expecting a proposal. None of them knew what she had been wishing for and none of them knew how her world had been totally turned on its head.

The girls took up their positions on the couches surrounding her.

'You look terrible,' Tilly said in her usual no-nonsense fashion. 'What's going on?'

In a house of four women, and one, often-absent, male, there weren't many secrets. Ellie didn't intend withholding the story but she didn't know if she was capable of sharing it tonight. She gathered the corners of the quilt in her hands and pulled it tight around her, seeking comfort in its warmth. She looked at each of her friends in turn. Her voice wobbled when she spoke. 'You'll say you told me so.'

'Of course we won't,' Jess said.

Ellie kept her focus on Jess. Tilly and Ruby had never really warmed to Rob and therefore Ellie thought Jess would be the most sympathetic. 'Rob asked me to dinner tonight and I was sure he was going to propose, but he had a different surprise.' She paused as she reached for a tissue and blew her nose. 'It turns out he's married.'

'What?'

'He's married?'

'That bastard,' Tilly fumed. 'I always had a bad feeling about him.'

'That's not helping,' Jess said to Tilly, before turning back to Ellie. 'Start at the beginning, tell us what happened.'

Ellie sniffed and reached for another tissue. 'Rob invited me to dinner and I was sure it was going to be a turning point in our relationship. You know how he doesn't like to go out on dates, he prefers to stay home, always saying he wants to relax after his long days at work and doesn't want his private life made public at the hospital.' The girls were nodding, they all knew Rob. He was an orthopaedic surgeon at Eastern Beaches Hospital where they all worked as nurses.

Ellie had accepted Rob's reasons as legitimate but now she wondered how many of them had been for convenience and deceit. 'I thought that because we were actually going out tonight it meant he was ready to go public with our relationship. I thought it was a good sign and I was all ready for a proposal or at least for him to ask me to move in with him. But he had an even bigger surprise. His wife and daughter arrive from the UK next week.'

'He has a daughter too?'

'And you had no idea?'

'Of course not,' Ellie protested. 'Do you think I would willingly have a relationship with a married man?'

'No,' Ruby said as she shook her head, 'but how do you keep something like that hidden?'

'Easy,' said Tilly, 'you keep them in another country.'

'But surely he'd have photos of them, take phone calls from them, stuff like that,' Jess mused.

'I guess with the time difference and his hours at the hospital it was easy to make sure he never spoke to them when I was around,' Ellie said. 'There was nothing to make me suspect he was anything other than what he said. There were no phone calls, he didn't wear a wedding ring and there were no family photos, not one.'

'Did he say why they're coming now? He's been here for months.'

'They were waiting until the end of the school year.'

'How old is his daughter?'

'Dunno.' Ellie shrugged. Getting all the details hadn't been high on her list of priorities. 'Old enough to go to school, I guess.'

'So he's just been killing time, fooling around with you, until his wife gets here?' Ruby sounded horrified.

'I always knew there was something suspicious about him.' Tilly sounded as though she'd like a chance to tear Rob to pieces.

'Well, you'll love the next bit even more,' Ellie told her, thinking it would give Tilly further reason to dislike Rob. 'He seemed to think I'd like to keep the relationship going once his wife arrived.'

'You're kidding! I hope you set him straight.'

'Of course. I actually created quite a scene. I didn't think I had it in me. I think that's why he orchestrated to have the conversation in a public place—I'm sure he thought there'd be safety in numbers.' Thinking back to her reaction, Ellie was rather pleased she'd shown some fight. Even if the whole experience had left her feeling em-barrassed and nauseous, at least she'd had the last word. And, as depressing as the evening had been, she did feel marginally better once she'd shared the saga with her girlfriends. 'I can't be-lieve I've been such an idiot.'

'It's not your fault, Ellie. Rob lied to you,' Ruby tried to console her.

'God, his poor wife,' said Tilly.

'Who cares about his wife! What about Ellie?' Jess was outraged.

Tilly just shrugged. 'Ellie is better off without him. His wife isn't so lucky, she's stuck with him.'

'But you guys know how much I want to

belong to someone,' Ellie said as she reached for yet another tissue. 'I had all my hopes pinned on Rob and he's played me for a complete fool.'

'Rob is the fool, Ellie,' Ruby interjected. 'Don't waste your time crying over him. You'll meet someone else, someone who deserves you.'

Jess agreed. 'Your soul mate is out there and he's worth waiting for. Then everything will fall into place. You'll have your happy ever after.'

'I thought he might be "the one".'

'Trust me, Ellie, he's not. You'll know when you meet "the one". You won't be left wondering.' Ruby had found her true love in Cort and she was convinced everyone else should, and would, experience the same happiness.

'I feel like I'm running out of time.'

'For goodness' sake, you're only twenty-three.' Tilly spoke up with the wisdom her few extra years gave her.

'I know, but I want children. You know I was an IVF baby—what if I have trouble getting pregnant, like my parents did? I want to know sooner rather than later.'

'If you want my advice, I wouldn't advertise

that fact. It's likely to scare most men away.' Tilly was her usual pragmatic self.

'If they don't want children then they're not the man for me, are they?' Ellie responded.

'But wanting children doesn't automatically make them right for you and I don't think you'll find most men putting kids at the top of their to-do list, even the decent ones.'

Ellie could feel tears welling up again. 'Rob said he wanted kids.'

'Now you know why. He's already got one.' Tilly in particular didn't keep her opinions to herself. Ellie loved Tilly dearly but she was definitely a person who saw the world in two dimensions—right and wrong—and unless you agreed with her you were obviously wrong! This made her a very good person to have in your corner but you didn't want to be on her bad side. She hadn't liked Rob and it turned out she'd been right about him all along.

'Tilly, a little sympathy wouldn't go astray,' Jess suggested.

Tilly reached around the bulky quilt and

hugged Ellie. 'I'm sorry you're upset now but things will work out. I know they will.'

'How on earth am I going to work with him?' Ellie asked as she blew her nose again.

'You go to work with your head held high. You've done nothing wrong. *He* lied to you.'

CHAPTER ONE

ELLIE'S eyes were stinging and she could feel tears welling up, accompanied by an unexpected lump in her throat as the coffin slid soundlessly on the stainless-steel rollers and disappeared through the curtain. Behind the curtain, screened from the mourners in the chapel, her grandmother's body would be taken away and all that would remain would be able to be contained in a small urn. That urn would end up behind a small brass plaque, next to the ashes of Ellie's grandfather and parents.

'You okay?'

Jess was sitting to Ellie's left. She was holding out a pack of tissues.

Ellie took one and smiled. 'Yes, I'm okay.' Her grandmother had been eighty-eight years old and her death hadn't been unexpected but it did mean that Ellie was now truly alone, the sole remaining member of her family. She was an only child and her parents had been killed when she was eleven. Her maternal grandparents had been her guardians and now they were both gone too. Her tears were selfish ones.

Surrounding her, flanking her, protecting her, were her closest friends. Jessica and Ruby sat on her left, Tilly on her right. She and Jess had been friends for several years now since meeting at university where they'd studied nursing together. They'd gone through the highs and lows of good and bad results, good and bad relationships and good and bad times generally. Ruby and Tilly had become her friends more recently, since they'd all started sharing a house and working at Eastern Beaches Hospital. These three were like family to her but they *weren't* family.

As she waited for the funeral music to stop playing Ellie thought back over the past two months. In the space of nine weeks she'd lost her boyfriend—well, not so much lost as found out he was actually someone else's cheating husband—and now she'd lost her grandmother. True, she had her friends but they weren't what she longed for. Her friends were fabulous but they weren't enough. Ellie wanted to belong and she longed for a family to call her own. Stop being pathetic, she told herself. It was one thing to cry over the death of a loved one, that was allowed, expected even, but to sit here, at her grandmother's funeral, feeling sorry for herself was being a little too self-indulgent. She was twenty-three years old, she had friends, she would be fine.

But the empty spot in her heart refused to listen. Ever since her parents had died she'd been conscious of this space waiting to be filled. She knew it could only be filled by love but it was a spot for family and family alone. No matter how much she loved her friends that spot was still there, empty, waiting. What if she never found her soul mate, her one true love. What if she never had the family she dreamed of? What if that empty spot was never filled?

Ellie shook her head. She couldn't think like that. She had to be strong. She had to be positive. Somewhere her perfect partner waited for her, she had to believe that. Rob had been a mistake, it didn't mean her quest for love was over. At least she hoped not.

The curtain was closed, the music had stopped, the coffin was gone, and her grandmother too. There was nothing left to do here.

She stood and her friends stood with her. They moved en masse to the lounge for the afternoon tea and shadowed her as she spoke to the funeral director and some of her grandmother's friends, keeping a silent and protective eye on her until Ellie decided that she was able to leave without seeming rude.

'Stat Bar, anyone?' Tilly suggested as they made their way out of the funeral home. The Stat Bar was their favourite after-work haunt; a few hundred metres down the hill from the hospital where they all worked and only a few steps from the house they all called home, it was convenient and trendy.

'Would you rather go somewhere else?' Ruby asked Ellie. 'Somewhere you can be anonymous?'

Ellie knew the Stat Bar would be crowded with hospital staff and she knew her friends would understand if she wanted to avoid it today but she shook her head. 'No, that sounds good. I'm fine, really.' A few familiar faces weren't going to bother her.

The sun was still shining when they got back to Coogee Beach on Sydney's south-eastern shore. It was a glorious afternoon, something Ellie couldn't reconcile with a funeral. But, she decided as she sipped her drink, the sun did boost her spirits.

They'd managed to grab a coveted outside table overlooking the beach and the tangy smell of salt in the air, the crisp white sand framing the ocean and the sound of the waves breaking on the shore all conspired to make her feel better. Maybe the fact she was on her second vodka, lime and soda was also helping to improve her mood.

The Stat Bar was beginning to fill up with the after-work crowd. The allied health practitioners from the hospital were the first to file through the doors, followed by the junior doctors. As more people gathered in the bar Ellie decided it was time to freshen her make-up, she could only imagine the state of her foundation and mascara. She stood up, hauling her bag from under her chair.

Her high heels clicked on the tiled floor as she entered the ladies' room. She always wore heels when she wasn't at work as a way of compensating for only being five feet two inches tall. She dumped her bag on the counter and examined her face. Her eyes were a bit bloodshot but not too swollen, although the tip of her nose was still red from crying. She pulled a hairbrush and her make-up out from the depths of her handbag. Tipping her head back, she squeezed a couple of eye drops into the corner of each eye before sliding the Alice band from her shoulder-length blonde hair and running the brush through it. She repositioned the Alice band, using it to hold her hair off her face as she blended a little foundation over her nose. She leant forward, overbalancing slightly on her high heels as she checked her eyes. The drops were working, her blue eyes looked a little brighter now. She straightened up and applied a fresh coat of gloss to her lips. She removed a few long blonde hairs from her black dress, checking to see that she'd gotten rid of all the stray strands.

As she walked past the bar to return to her

friends she saw Rob, her lying, adulterous ex, paying for his drinks. His distinctive appearance made him easy to pick out in a crowd. He was out of his theatre clothes and was wearing an immaculately pressed suit, a sharp contrast to the more casual clothes and various hospital uniforms that surrounded him. He had his back to the ocean and to the rest of the room and she could pass behind him unseen. She hurried past as Rob picked up his drink and turned from the bar.

'Rob's here,' Ruby pointed out when Ellie returned to their table.

'I saw him.'

'Are you happy to stay?'

Ellie nodded, 'Yes, I'm fine. Completely recovered.'

She'd had to recover quickly. She and Rob worked together on the orthopaedic ward so she saw him on an almost daily basis and she hadn't had the luxury of time to retreat to lick her wounds in privacy. She'd had to maintain a civil working relationship. Rob's personality was aloof and cool at the best of times, something

Tilly had always delighted in reminding Ellie of, and since the breakdown of their relationship he certainly hadn't become any more amenable, but mostly they managed to work together harmoniously. Although she didn't want to socialise with him, she had no problem being in the same bar as him.

'I'm still embarrassed,' she admitted, 'but pleased the whole thing was such a secret that I don't have to live out my embarrassment in front of the entire hospital. I know I got caught up in all the possibilities of the relationship but I think I might have learnt my lesson, for a while at least. I'm going to take my time from now on, not dive in head first.'

Ellie's remark made Ruby grin and Tilly laughed.

'What's so funny?' Ellie demanded.

'Famous last words,' Tilly replied. 'I've never known anyone who falls in love as quickly as you.'

'I admit I'm a hopeless romantic,' Ellie replied to Tilly, 'and when you fell in love with Marcus, and Ruby and Cort sorted out their lives, I got a bit carried away, thinking I could be next, but I'm going to be patient.' She reminded herself that she was going to be strong. Positive. Her perfect partner was out there, she just had to bide her time. She would find someone. 'There's someone out there for me and when the time is right he'll appear.'

'How about right now?' Jess interrupted. 'There's a hot guy at the bar.'

'I didn't mean today.' Ellie laughed.

'Check him out before you cross him off your list,' Jess advised. 'He looks okay to me.'

Ellie turned her head. It wasn't hard to see who Jess was talking about. Leaning on the bar, wearing faded jeans and a snug black T-shirt that hugged his sculpted arms and chest, was one definitely hot guy. He had one foot on the railing that ran around the base of the bar and his jeans were moulded to his very shapely back-side. He was thin, not scrawny, but his waist was narrow. There was no sign of any spread around his middle and Ellie could see a slight ripple of abdominal muscles along his side. He looked naturally slim, not like he spent hours in the gym.

His face was in profile as he waited for his order. He had a square jaw darkened by a hint of stubble, full lips, one dark eyebrow that she could see and dark lashes. He got his order and turned away from them, unaware of their scrutiny as he moved through the crowd. Ellie straightened in her seat and followed his progress across the room. His walk was quite graceful, his long lean lines leant fluidity to his move-ment, and his steps were confident. He stopped to join the group of surgeons standing with Rob and Ellie watched, intrigued, as Rob introduced him to the others. How did Rob know him?

'Do you know who he is?' Jess asked. She'd shifted in her chair to get a better look.

'No idea,' Ellie replied.

She had a good view of him now. Standing beside Rob, she could see he was a few inches shorter, around six feet tall. Rob was getting thicker around his middle and the contrast be-tween Hot Guy and Rob made Rob look older than his thirty-three years. Rob's hair was more grey than brown, although it was still thick. Hot Guy had thick, almost black hair, with a definite curl.

'If Ellie isn't interested, you should go and introduce yourself, Jess,' Ruby suggested.

Ellie couldn't remember saying she wasn't interested in the hot guy specifically but she bit her tongue because she had just said she was going to bide her time.

'No way. I'm not going to interrupt that group,' Jess said.

Ellie understood her sentiments. As very recent nursing graduates they still felt there was a pecking order among the medical staff and their social standing in the hospital certainly didn't allow them to fraternise with the surgeons uninvited out of hours. And if the group of surgeons included Rob, they'd definitely keep their distance.

But Ellie knew there was another reason why Jess wouldn't approach the hot guy. Jess had been quite genuine in pointing him out to Ellie and even if he hadn't been talking to Rob she wouldn't have gone over, because Jess was completely besotted with Adam.

Adam Carmichael; the token male in their house, their mostly absent landlord, Ruby's brother and their resident Casanova rolled into one. There was never a shortage of women traipsing through his door when he was in Sydney and the girls often joked that he should put a revolving door on his bedroom so he could move his conquests in and out more efficiently. And, even though he was completely wrong for her, Jess had a thing for Adam.

Ellie wished Jess would meet somebody who would take her mind off him, someone who was ready for a real relationship, someone who wouldn't break her heart. But despite Ellie's pleas Jess seemed quite determined to ignore any other possibilities, including the hot guy. And in that case, Ellie decided, *she* might as well enjoy the view.

She looked back into the bar. Hot Guy was still talking to Rob but he was looking at her. Their gazes locked and something flashed through her. A jolt, a strike, a shock to the heart, and the rest of the room receded as the spark of connection flared. She sat still, riveted to the spot as he looked her up and down without a hint of embarrassment. She should have been horrified but all she could do was wait for him to finish. Wait for his eyes to meet hers again. Without consciously acknowledging her actions, she was waiting to see if she could work out what had happened with that first glance. What was it?

His gaze returned to her face and there it was again. A flash of what? Recognition? Ellie wondered if he knew who she was. She mentally shook her head. No. Rob would never have talked about her.

She didn't move, she couldn't move. She knew she was staring but she couldn't stop. She felt a blush spread up her neck and into her cheeks but still she couldn't look away.

His smouldering good looks had a slight wildness about them, an edginess, which drew her to him. She imagined she could feel the heat radiating from him. Her fingers itched to touch him and if he'd been standing beside her she knew she would have reached out to feel him.

She could imagine the heat of his hands burning her skin and that made her blush even more.

He held her gaze, a hint of mischief in his eyes, almost as though he could read her thoughts, and then he grinned at her. Ellie smiled back. She didn't mean to and she was surprised to find her face was capable of expression but her smile was an automatic response to the power of his.

She tore her eyes away from his, forcing herself to break the connection. She tried to focus on the conversation going on around her, tried to behave normally, tried to pretend she hadn't just shared a moment with a hot stranger.

She had no idea how successful she was being but thankfully the arrival of Ruby's fiancé, Cort, provided a welcome distraction.

Cort was a senior emergency registrar and Ellie wondered if he knew who the hot guy was. She didn't have to wonder for long.

'Do you know who the guy in the black T-shirt is over there? The one who's talking to Rob Coleman?' Ruby inclined her head in their direction as she asked Cort the question.

'That's James Leonardi,' he said as he took in the group. 'He's a new registrar.'

'In Emergency?' Ellie asked. Was the new reg working with Cort?

Cort shook his head. 'Orthopaedics.'

'Orthopaedics?' Ellie repeated. She didn't know whether to be nervous or delighted. The hot guy was an orthopod? She was going to have to work with him?

'He's transferred from Royal North Shore. I understand the director of orthopaedics poached him, and apparently there are high expectations of him.'

Ellie was vaguely aware that Cort was still talking but her mind had wandered off in the direction of the hot guy. James Leonardi. His name sounded Spanish or Italian. She should have known. That would explain where the heat was coming from, he would have passionate blood running through his veins, it was almost tangible. It was in his eyes too, in the look he had given her. Fire, heat and passion.

There was a silent humming in the air around her. She could feel it and she was convinced it was coming from him. How was it possible to feel such an instant connection with a complete stranger?

She shifted in her chair. She needed to change position. She needed something else to look at. She was going to be working with the man so she needed to picture him in a white coat, in a sterile environment. In theatre scrubs. No. That wasn't helping. He looked just as good in her imagination.

Maybe she should go home. Maybe it was a case of out of sight, out of mind.

CHAPTER TWO

ELLIE stepped into the shower and tried to let the water wash away thoughts of Dr James Leonardi. Out of sight, out of mind hadn't worked terribly well. He'd been in her dreams all night. Her subconscious had been infiltrated by a stranger.

But he didn't feel like a stranger.

She closed her eyes and his image burst into her head. She could instantly recall the line of his shoulder under his T-shirt, the slight curl in his black hair and the heat in his expression when he'd looked at her with his dark eyes. She let her memory linger on the curve of his butt and the long sinewy length of his back as she rinsed her hair before she opened her eyes, turned off the shower and attempted to banish all further thoughts of him from her mind. She needed to focus. She had to work with him. She couldn't let her fantasies rule her thoughts.

And a fantasy was all he could be. She wasn't going to date another doctor. She wasn't going to make that mistake again. It was too awkward when things went badly. She'd learnt that much from her experience with Rob. The orthopaedic ward was definitely off limits and, therefore, so was James Leonardi.

But putting him out of her mind was easier said than done. Especially as he was all anyone wanted to talk about at handover that morning.

'Have you seen the new doctor?'

'Yep.'

'Isn't he superb?'

'Is he Italian? He looks Italian.'

'I was on yesterday when he started and he's as Australian as you and me.'

'Oh, you lucky thing. Is he as gorgeous as he looks?'

Listening to the nurses' gossip, it was as though the outside world had ceased to exist. This new world appeared to revolve entirely around Dr James Leonardi. Ellie kept quiet. She had nothing to contribute, she hadn't actually met or spoken to him, and her thoughts were not for sharing.

The CNC handed Ellie a stack of files. 'You can accompany Dr. Leonardi on his rounds this morning—you know the patients better than anyone. I've given you George, Mavis, Dylan and Jenny.'

Ellie wondered if she'd been given this job because of her silence rather than her nursing skills. Not that it mattered. She took the files and went to wait for the rest of the group.

Ward rounds in a teaching hospital tended to be rather large affairs. They would be accompanied by the ward physio, Charlotte, and however many physio students she'd have with her today. There were nursing students on the ward too and there would possibly be a medical student or two and an intern. It was rather daunting for the patients until they got used to it and daunting for the students also.

All the chatter from the other nurses still hadn't prepared Ellie for the jolt she got when she saw Dr Leonardi again. Her first official encounter with him was hardly going to be an intimate affair but that didn't stop her heart from racing with expectation. He watched her intently as she introduced herself.

'Dr. Leonardi, I'm Ellie Nicholson, I'll be doing your rounds with you this morning.' As she spoke she was aware of that strange connection again, that silent hum, that unexplained feeling that he knew more about her than he should, and she could see in his eyes that he remembered her.

'Hello again,' he said, and although his gaze didn't move from her face Ellie felt as though he was running his eyes over the length of her just as he'd done yesterday in the Stat Bar. His eyes were dark, dark brown and by the look in them she knew he was recalling yesterday too. She felt another blush creep up her neck as the corners of his eyes creased as he smiled and his eyes darkened further, reminding her of molten chocolate.

He extended his hand. It was warm, just as she'd expected, and now she could feel that silent hum pulsing up her arm. It was no longer just moving through the air, it was moving through her and it was definitely coming from him. She could feel herself wanting to close her eyes, wanting to lose herself in the force field that surrounded them. That was the only way to describe the sensation. She fought to keep her eyes open, fought not to succumb to his intensity.

She felt Charlotte watching her and knew she was wondering about Dr Leonardi's choice of words. *Hello again.*

She avoided the physio's gaze as she fought to keep a level head. She let go of Dr Leonardi's hand as she checked to see if the right people had assembled.

'Shall we get started?' she said, turning away from James Leonardi and forcing herself to concentrate as she led the group to the first patient on her list. Her job would be to make sure that all the medical staff was up to speed on the patient's condition and treatment regime. Charlotte would be responsible for ensuring that the physio angle was covered and together they would work out what else needed to be done or discuss discharge possibilities.

'Morning, George,' Ellie greeted their first

patient, before introducing him to the group and handing his case notes to James. She took a step closer to the bed, putting some distance between her and James. She had to move away, it was impossible to stay focussed on her work when he stood so near. He smelt like limes, like a cool drink on a hot day, and she was finding him hugely distracting.

'This is George Poni,' she said, forcing herself to concentrate on the patient. 'He's a fifty-year-old who came off second best when his motorbike hit a guard rail six days ago. He sustained a fractured left ankle, left head of radius, clavicle and wrist. He underwent open reduction, internal fixation of his ankle and wrist and conservative, non-surgical treatment of his clavicle and elbow. He's had no complications and we're starting to consider discharge.'

'I can't go home,' George interrupted. 'My wife is going to kill me. Tell them, Ellie.'

'You'll be fine, George,' Ellie said in an attempt to placate him. 'I've spoken to Lilly and she's quite calm about the whole thing now as long as you promise to give up the motorbike and find some other safer hobby to pursue through your mid-life crisis. Her words, not mine!' she added at the end of her spiel. Out of the corner of her eye she could see James smiling. His smile was wide and it brought creases to the corners of his eyes. He had the smile of someone who smiled often and who was used to people smiling with him.

'Other than putting his life in danger, is there any other reason not to discharge George?' James asked. 'How mobile is he, Charlotte?'

'He's partial weight-bearing on his left leg and can manage short distances with one crutch, but we're planning on sending him home with a wheelchair as he can't use two crutches because of his upper-limb injuries. There's still a lot of swelling but nothing more than expected. Despite George's protestations, his wife is capable and willing to give support.'

James was checking the medication chart at the end of George's bed. 'He's still having four-hourly Panadeine Forte?' He directed his question at Ellie.

'For his elbow and ankle.' Ellie clarified George's pain relief requirements.

'Do we need this bed?'

'No.' Ellie shook her head. 'We're okay at the moment.'

'Okay, George. I'll do you a deal. Let's see how you go with painkillers every six hours but we'll start making arrangements for discharge and review your situation tomorrow.'

'Thanks, Doc.'

'Next?' James said. Ellie indicated the bed diagonally opposite George's, where a very thin, pale young man lay, and the group migrated to his bedside.

'Dylan Harris, twenty-four, also involved in a motorbike accident, six weeks ago. He sustained a fractured right femur and fractured pelvis. He's had a K-nail inserted into his femur and was in traction for his pelvis. He been a bit slow to get up and get moving.' In fact, if she was being totally honest, Ellie would say Dylan was being ridiculously pathetic. He regularly burst into dramatic tears whenever the physios came to do his treatment, even though his injuries were healing well and there was nothing to be concerned about from his recovery point of view.

'What seems to be the problem?'

'A lack of motivation and co-operation,' Charlotte contributed.

'I'm not using that walking frame, that's for old people,' Dylan sulked, indicating the gutter frame that was waiting beside his bed.

Charlotte sighed. 'How many times have we had this conversation, Dylan? The rate you're going you *will* be old before you get out of here. Once I'm confident that you're walking safely with the frame we can look at progressing to crutches.'

'I'll get up if Ellie walks with me.'

'You have to walk with the physios first,' Charlotte replied. 'It's hospital policy.'

'Why don't I come back with Charlotte after rounds and we'll get you out of bed together?' Ellie suggested. 'I'll be your second person assist,' she said to Charlotte.

'As long as you're sure,' Charlotte said.

Ellie didn't really have time to spend getting Dylan on his feet for the first time. She knew how long that process could take. Even just a few steps would be a massive task when he'd been lying in bed for so long. But there didn't seem to be any other way this was going to happen. She nodded.

'Any other issues?' James asked.

'None,' Ellie replied.

'All right. Dylan, if I come back tomorrow and find you haven't at least attempted to get out of bed I'll get you moved to another ward where you won't have Ellie *or* Charlotte looking after you,' James threatened, obviously figuring that was the way to get Dylan motivated. 'But if you start complying with treatment you can stay here.'

By the look on Dylan's face Ellie could tell he wasn't sure whether he'd just won the argument or been gazumped by Dr Leonardi. In Ellie's opinion it was Dr Leonardi 1, Dylan 0.

When James finished his rounds and left the ward Ellie felt as though he'd taken some of her energy with him, although a hint of his fresh lime scent remained, tantalising her senses.

She threw herself into the morning's work, hoping that if she kept busy she wouldn't have time to think about Dr Leonardi. Wouldn't have time to think about his chocolate eyes and how they'd watched every move she'd made. Wouldn't have time to think about those full lips and how they'd curled into a smile when she'd said something that had amused him, and she wouldn't have time to think about the throbbing she felt in the air when she was near him or the way it pulsed through her body when he touched her.

In some ways she hoped his effect on her would wear off as he spent more time on the ward. Maybe it would fade away and she'd be able to work in peace. But a part of her enjoyed the buzz he gave her, the feeling of danger, as though he was forbidden fruit.

Maybe that was the attraction, the exact thing that had got people into trouble all through the ages—wanting something they *couldn't* have. After her disastrous fling with Rob she wasn't going to get involved with someone on the orthopaedic ward again. Not ever.

She'd just have to ignore those feelings, she told herself. That would be the sensible thing to do.

'Ellie? Are you awake?'

'Come in, Jess.'

The door opened. 'Good, you're up. Do you want to come for a walk with me?'

Ellie looked at her watch. Ten past eight.

'Now?' she said.

'Please,' Jess begged as she pulled Ellie's curtains back. 'Adam's home again and I don't want to be here when he gets up.'

Now the early morning walk made sense. Ellie knew Jess wouldn't want to confront whoever it was who had kept Adam company last night. Their house belonged to Adam and the fifth bedroom was his to use whenever he was in Sydney. His work as a surgeon with Operation New Faces had him travelling around the world but when he was home there was always an endless stream of girls in and out of his bed, and Ellie knew Jess found that upsetting. Being reminded of Adam's casual attitude to relationships was almost more than Jess could handle and she hated having to play nice whenever her path crossed with one of his many women.

'Okay,' Ellie conceded, 'give me a minute to get dressed.' Her room was flooded with light. It was going to be a beautiful day and she may as well get up and enjoy it. She climbed out of bed and pulled on underwear, a sports singlet and shorts. She'd shower later. She went to the mirror to brush her hair and tied it back into a ponytail. She rubbed sunscreen over her skin and grabbed a hat and her sunglasses. She was ready.

A light northerly breeze was blowing along the foreshore as Ellie and Jess crossed Arden Street and headed for the path that hugged the beach. The morning sun was warm on Ellie's skin with enough heat in it to make the breeze feel pleasant instead of uncomfortable.

A low stone wall separated the beach from the path and Ellie and Jess had to dodge joggers and dog walkers as they headed north. At this early hour the only people who were up were people who had a reason to be—people who wanted to get their morning exercise in or who had young children. The lawn area was teeming with families and there were even some keen ones on the beach, building sandcastles and swimming.

Ellie kept her gaze averted from the young families. She didn't need a reminder of what she was missing. Since breaking up with Rob, she'd decided she would bide her time before starting another relationship. She'd had a few intense, short-lived relationships in the past year and she'd thought having a self-enforced break would be a good idea.

'Perhaps I should get a dog,' she said to Jess.

'What are you talking about?'

Ellie waved a hand in the general direction of the other pedestrians. 'Everyone here has either got kids or a dog. If I'm not going to have kids, maybe a dog is a good alternative. Lots of people do that.'

'Since when aren't you having kids?' Jess asked.

'Well, I won't be having any in the near future so a dog might be a good alternative,' she explained. 'Besides you know how, when you want something really badly, it seems to take for ever to happen and how, if you stop wanting it, it falls into your lap? Maybe, if I decide to get a dog, I'll meet the man who will be the father of my children just because I've replaced the idea of kids with the reality of a dog.'

'I don't get that logic at all,' Jess replied, and Ellie caught her sideways look, the one that said she thought her friend might be going mad. 'I think we need to walk a bit faster. We need to get to Bondi and see the backpackers—the young, single crowd who don't have kids *or* a dog. That's another reality, you know. Anyway, I thought you were taking a break from the dating scene.'

'I am,' Ellie replied, but even as she uttered the words she knew she could be tempted out of her self-imposed ban very quickly and it was all because of James Leonardi. Since he'd arrived at Eastern Beaches, on the orthopaedic ward, her hormones had gone into overdrive. She was overwhelmingly aware of him and his presence reminded her that she loved being in a relation-ship. Loved the idea of being in love. 'I think what I'm trying to say is that perhaps if I stop trying to find my ideal man, he might find me.'

Jess nodded. 'That makes a bit more sense but, you know what, I think you might just need to revise your definition of your perfect man. You might not want to hear this but I think you've been looking at the wrong type of men.'

'What do you mean?'

'You've always gone for the guys who appeared sensible and mature, older than you, ones who you think might be ready to settle down, without really worrying about what they're like. Maybe you should try dating someone your own age.'

'What's age got to do with it? Cort's older than Ruby and you're still lusting after Adam, who's older than you too, why do I have to date the young ones?' Ellie argued.

'Maybe not too young but maybe you should look for someone who's not so serious and staid, someone who knows how to have a good time, less of a father figure.'

Ellie frowned. 'Is that what you think I've been doing?'

'I think you're looking for someone to be the father of your children but I also think you want someone who will take care of you,' Jess explained. 'You don't need that, you can take care of yourself. I think you should choose a man because he's a good man, not because you think he'll make a good father. Look for someone who you can have a bit of fun with. You don't need to rush into the whole marriage and babies thing. You're still young. Relax.' Jess stopped talking as they walked up a steep stretch of path but as soon as they were on a downhill slope again she continued. 'If I told you your ideal man was waiting around the corner for you, tell me what you'd want to see.'

That was easy. 'Taller than me,' Ellie said, 'maybe a *bit* older, fit but not with weightlifter muscles, more of a runner's physique.' So what if her description was an identical match to James Leonardi? Surely there were plenty of other men who could be described in the same fashion!

'And what would he be like?'

'What do you mean?'

'Well, does he make you laugh or does he take

life very seriously? Could he be divorced? Already have kids? Do you want a professional or someone who has a job where they get dirty? A dog person or a cat person? Tea or coffee drinker?'

They'd reached Gordon's Bay and turned for the trip home. As they walked down the hill around the northern end of Coogee Bay, past Rob's apartment building, Ellie quickened her pace, not slowing until they'd made it back to the stone wall that signalled the beginning of the beach. A few fishing boats were being taken out from the fishing club and there were a couple of games of beach volleyball under way. Ellie's attention was drawn to a game of two on two between four fit young guys. They were all wearing board shorts without shirts, their bodies tanned and firm in the morning sun. A few steps closer and Ellie's heart began to race in her chest. There was something familiar about one of them.

Olive skin, dark hair, a lithe frame. Her fictitious ideal man. James Leonardi.

He had his back to them and his calf muscles

bulged as he propelled himself off the sand and into the air to block a ball at the net. His block was successful and Ellie watched as he high-fived his partner and waited for the ball to be returned. He scooped it up and prepared to serve. He tossed the ball high and raised his arms in the air as he hit it over the net. Ellie could see the muscles of his back ripple with the movement. She'd seen his face in profile as he'd served the ball over the net but, even without that glimpse, Ellie knew it was him, she could feel it. That humming in the air was back, getting louder as she got closer. Her senses were on high alert. The sun was a bit brighter, the tang of the sea a bit saltier, the air a bit warmer, but the sounds of the other people had faded a little. The humming was drowning the other sounds out.

'Well? What do you think?' Jess was still waiting for Ellie to answer her questions.

Without a trace of a doubt Ellie knew what she wanted. He was right there, in front of her.

As vaguely as she could, she answered Jess's last question. She tried not to watch James as she spoke but it was hard to keep her attention focussed elsewhere. 'He has a smile that could brighten any day. He should have a job he enjoys but he doesn't necessarily have to wear a suit and a tie to work. He needs to like being active, a physical kind of guy, but he'd have to smell nice. He needs a sense of humour and he needs to love his family. He doesn't need to have his life all mapped out but he would need to know how to treat a woman and he must be prepared to only date one woman at a time.'

Ellie wasn't sure if James qualified for any of those things, for all she knew he was already married with half a dozen children, but surely with that smouldering, Latin thing he had going on, not to mention the look he had in his eye, she was willing to bet he'd taken his fair share of women to bed, and she was willing, if he was available, to put her hand up to join that list. He could be her experiment, she decided. She could try choosing a man first and looking for a father for her future children second. She could live in the moment for a change. She didn't have to fall in love with him.

She managed to position herself between Jess

and the beach so she was able to keep one eye on the volleyball, and on James, as they walked past. With her hair tied back and hidden underneath a cap she didn't think he'd recognise her so she thought she could check him out from behind her dark glasses. As they drew level he bent down to pick up the ball and Ellie felt safe enough to let her eyes run over him. His shorts pulled taut over his legs and butt as he squatted down to the sand and his biceps flexed as he retrieved the ball. As he straightened up he looked directly at her. Ellie had thought he wouldn't recognise her but he paused in mid-action and stood still, only for a second or two but Ellie knew that in that space of time he'd known it was her. She quickly averted her gaze and hurried past. She felt as though he could read her mind and she definitely did not want him to know what she was thinking.

She kept walking, resisting the urge to turn around as she and Jess continued on to the kiosk by the beach stairs where they stopped for coffee. While they waited for their orders to be filled she wondered whether she'd lost her mind. She was supposed to be getting her life into order and taking stock of her goals, not thinking about ripping the clothes of a virtual stranger.

She must be mad to think about James Leonardi at all. Dating was supposed to be off her list and dating another doctor from the same department would definitely be asking for trouble. But there was something irresistible about him. Not just his looks or the powerful, passionate vibe he exuded; it had something to do with that strange humming sensation, that magnetic pull that seemed to draw her to him. Even now, she knew she could turn around and instantly find him in a crowd. Somehow they were connected.

But she had to ignore these feelings. She kept her back turned to the beach as she waited for her coffee, resisting the urge to take just one more look. It didn't matter how much she fancied him, James Leonardi was not for her.

CHAPTER THREE

WHEN Ellie returned to work on Tuesday it was to one of the worst shifts she'd had in a long time and it was all thanks to Rob. Mostly they'd managed to work amicably together since the demise of their affair but occasionally she seemed to be in his firing line and today was an especially bad day. She was being blamed for every little thing that went wrong—a dressing that hadn't been changed, X-rays that had been misplaced and a blood test that had been ordered but hadn't been done fast enough to please Rob. None of these things were actually Ellie's tasks, she was up to her neck in admissions and discharge summaries, but Rob had decided to haul her over hot coals for the failings of the entire ward. And he wasn't finished yet. Ellie was completing paperwork at the nurses' station when she saw him marching towards her with a severe expression on his face. She froze, wondering what she was going to be blamed for now.

He stopped a few paces from her and snapped. 'I just saw George Poni and his wife getting into the lift. He tells me he's going home.'

'Yes, I'm filing his paperwork now,' she said, waving a hand towards the stack of papers on the desk.

'Who said he was ready for discharge? Mr Poni is my patient.'

'Yes, but you handed his care over to Dr. Leonardi.' Ellie tried to keep a neutral tone.

'I still expect the courtesy of being informed if my patients are leaving.'

First I've heard of it, Ellie thought, but she bit her tongue. 'I'm sorry, I didn't realise you wanted everything discussed with you. The physio said he was ready to leave, his mobility aids and equipment for home have been organised, I've made an outpatient appointment for George to see you in a fortnight and his discharge was discussed with Dr Leonardi,' she explained. She was tired of being made a scapegoat for Rob's bad mood today.

'Next time I would like to be kept in the loop,' Rob barked at her. 'I expect to have my orders followed. Is that understood?'

I was following orders, Ellie felt like saying. *You hadn't indicated that James wasn't to discharge your patients.* She knew the appropriate discharge procedures had been followed. 'Yes, Dr Coleman,' she replied, hoping he'd go away and leave her alone if she didn't argue. She couldn't believe he was treating her this way but she was powerless to prevent his verbal lashing and he knew it. Her meek and mild attitude had the desired effect. With one final glare in her direction Rob stormed from the ward.

'Boy, you're in his bad books today. I've never seen him that irritated.' Sarah, a first-year nursing graduate, who had been keeping her head down throughout Rob's tirade, spoke up the moment he left. 'What have you done to upset him?'

Ellie blinked back tears. She wasn't going to let him get to her. She knew exactly what she'd done to annoy him. She'd gone against his wishes and she knew Rob was annoyed over her refusal to continue their relationship but she couldn't believe he was choosing to take it out on her in this fashion. He had no cause to query her work performance; she was good at her job and she took pride in that. She knew what the problem was but there was nothing she could say, or do, that wouldn't put her in the spotlight. She couldn't tell anyone else why he was treating her this way. So she shrugged.

'Maybe he just got out of the wrong side of the bed,' she proposed.

'I see his mood hasn't improved at all.'

Ellie looked up from her paperwork at the sound of James's voice. How long had he been standing there, she wondered and what had he heard? She was only just feeling brave enough to face him after seeing him at the beach on the weekend and now he'd witnessed her latest embarrassing moment. She was ready to crawl under the desk at the thought that he'd heard that exchange with Rob.

'Any idea what that was all about?' he asked.

He was watching her with his chocolate gaze, seemingly oblivious to her discomfort.

'He was annoyed because George Poni has been discharged without his say-so,' Ellie told him.

James frowned, a crease marring his smooth olive forehead. 'I wonder why he didn't say anything to me about that.'

Ellie shrugged. 'Maybe I'm an easier target.' There was no reason for anyone to think that Rob's earlier behaviour was related to her in any way, shape or form, especially not if she appeared unfazed.

'He was biting people's heads off in Theatre too this morning so unless you did something to upset him before that I think you're off the hook,' James said.

And then he smiled at her, a wide smile that brought those lovely creases to the corners of his dark eyes. Instantly Ellie felt her confidence restored, just his presence helped to soothe her frazzled nerves and his smile almost completely eradicated all thoughts of Rob's tirade from her mind. That hum of electricity she could feel when he was present made everything else recede. Harsh words, colleagues, nothing else seemed to matter so much and once again Ellie had to force herself to concentrate on the tasks at hand.

She breathed a sigh of relief. 'So it's not just me, then.' She paused briefly and mentally crossed her fingers before asking, 'He didn't explain why he was so cross?'

'Are you kidding? He's an orthopaedic surgeon, he doesn't have to explain himself to anyone!'

Ellie closed the file she'd been working on and looked up at him. There were two bright spots of colour on her cheeks and her blue eyes were glistening but the panicked look he'd seen there a moment before had vanished. Her earlier nervous expression had been replaced by a smile as she laughed at his flippant comment.

'Are you here on a social call or is there someone you want to see?' she asked.

As she spoke her blonde hair bounced around her shoulders, catching the light and distracting him. Why had he come to the ward? He struggled to recall what he was doing there. 'I'm here to see Mavis Williams. I was paged, something about her temperature?'

Ellie nodded. 'Yep. Let me grab her file and I'll come with you.'

She collected the case notes and led the way and he trailed a couple of steps behind, enjoying the way her hips moved as she stepped out in front. She was a petite woman, several inches shorter than him but perfectly proportioned. Her waist was tiny, her hips narrow but they swayed enticingly.

She'd intrigued him since the first time he'd seen her at the Stat Bar and he'd celebrated his good fortune when he'd discovered that not only did she work at the hospital but she worked on the orthopaedic ward. She'd be working with him.

When he'd seen her at the Stat Bar it was as though they had been the only two people in the room. She'd been surrounded by others but it was as if they had receded into the distance, leaving her standing alone, silhouetted by her own golden glow. It had been an odd sensation for James.

He'd felt her presence at the beach too. It had been more than just the feeling you got when you knew you were being watched. There had been something extra. Despite her cap and sunglasses, he'd known instantly it was her. He'd felt her and it wasn't until she'd walked away that he'd noticed she wasn't alone. She may have been walking with a friend but he'd only had eyes for Ellie.

She was the first woman to catch his attention in months, in almost seven months to be exact. Perhaps he was ready to move on.

'Morning, Mavis,' James greeted the old lady as they entered her room. 'You're running a temperature, I hear.'

Ellie retook Mavis's temperature as James checked her other symptoms. 'The nurses might be right, Mavis. It's possible you have a UTI. It's a common complaint in hospitals, I'm afraid. If you can stomach cranberry juice that's often a good natural combatant but I'll organise some tests and if necessary we can treat it with antibiotics.' He glanced at Ellie, who immediately picked up on his silent request.

'I'll go and organise the things for the urine culture,' she said.

James watched her go. She made him think of summer and sunshine and happy times. She was golden and if he believed in auras that would be how he would describe her. She had a golden aura and it seemed to envelop him whenever he was near her. It ensnared him and made it difficult to think past her and just being around her made him feel good.

'You're enjoying your new job, I see?' Mavis said with a smile.

'It certainly has some perks.' He wasn't embarrassed at being caught watching Ellie. Most of the males on staff did the same, he'd seen them. Almost everyone seemed captivated by her and he wondered if she was aware of the effect she had on men.

'You're not married, then?'

He hadn't been embarrassed until Mavis made that remark. Did she think he'd still be watching Ellie if he were married? He shook his head. 'No. I never quite made it down the aisle.'

'Why don't you ask Ellie out? She's single too,' Mavis the matchmaker replied.

'Is she?' His heart rate increased with the announcement. 'How do you know that?'

'You don't get to my age without learning a thing or two about people and, besides, I've been here so long I'm starting to feel like part of the furniture and when people get used to having you around they forget to watch their conversations. Trust me, she's single. You should ask her out.'

'I might take your advice. Thanks, Mavis,' he said with a wink as Ellie returned to the room. But even as he spoke he wondered if he would issue an invitation. What would be the sensible thing to do? Had anything changed in his life over the past few months? He was still committed to his job, still focussed on establishing his career. Did he have the time or emotional energy for the singles scene? No matter how enticing Ellie was, he wasn't sure if he was ready to date again.

There was a buzz of excitement in the room. The noise level had been high all evening, as was usually the case in a room full of women, but the level had increased noticeably in the last few minutes. Ellie checked her watch—ten-thirty. Her school leavers' reunion had been girls only until now and her old school friends were becoming distracted by the arrival of their boyfriends.

They had only been out of school for five years so there wasn't all that much to catch up on. They'd been doing one of three things—travelling overseas, studying or working or a combination of all of those. A few were married, a couple had babies but they were the exceptions.

Ellie watched as Carol, Amy and Fiona, in fact, most of the organising committee, went to greet their partners as they entered the function room. Two things were immediately obvious to Ellie. One, that three hours was the time limit allocated to catching up with friends before the girls needed to let their partners in on the evening and, two, the committee members were all in relationships, which was why the decision to include partners in the evening had been made. A third thing came to mind as Ellie watched the change in group dynamics—she wasn't in the mood to watch happy couples.

It had been three months since the disastrous dinner with Rob and her heart was well and truly mended. If she was honest, she'd admit her pride and her ego had suffered more than her heart. It was more about her dreams and what his lies had done to them. She was angry more than heartbroken and it wasn't difficult to be angry with a man who was a liar and a cheat. Her dreams might have been shattered but her heart was intact, though she still didn't feel like being surrounded by happy couples.

The reunion was being held in Sydney's infamous Kings Cross district in a private function room in a recently renovated and refurbished building. The building was typical of many in the Cross, with the businesses making the most of limited land by going upwards. There was a 'gentleman's club' in the basement, a traditional nightclub on the ground floor with function rooms on the first floor, and Ellie didn't want to know what was on the floor above that.

The reunion committee had booked out the

function room until midnight and Ellie knew that gave them access to the nightclub afterwards. Normally she would be planning on partying until the small hours of the morning but tonight she was out of sorts. She was tired of the incessant noisy chatter going on about her but it was still too early to go home. To get some respite from the noise she slipped out of the room and onto the balcony that opened off it. Maybe watching people in the Cross, instead of her old school friends and their partners, would improve her mood.

She closed the balcony doors behind her and the change in atmosphere between inside and outside was incredible. Inside the air had smelt of perfume, hairspray and women and while initially that had been overpowering it was at least a clean smell. Outside the air smelt of petrol fumes, cigarettes, greasy takeaway food, alcohol and men. And the noise had changed from the high-pitched, excited chatter of women to car horns, music and deeper, loud voices.

If she had been down at street level she might have retreated inside but on a first-floor balcony she felt safe enough to watch from a distance. The balcony was divided in two by a low iron balustrade and a second function room opened onto the other half. From her vantage point Ellie could see people inside the other room but for the moment the adjoining balcony was empty.

She crossed the balcony and leant on the railing overlooking Darlinghurst Road. It was still early by Cross standards but the crowds were building. There were no queues outside the nightclubs yet; they were still advertising free entry and cheap drinks in an effort to entice patrons inside. There were the other enticements too and she could hear several men spruiking for customers as they promised visual, and other, delights. *'We have beautiful women, they will dance just for you!'*

Noise to her left caught her attention. A few guys had gathered on the adjacent balcony, beers in hand as they lit their cigarettes. They were all young—late twenties to early thirties at a guess and out of interest, and habit, she gave them a once-over. They weren't a bad-looking group, most of them looked reasonably fit, if you ignored the cigarettes, and neatly dressed. They were well groomed and looked educated and professional.

Through the open doors she now had a better view into the other function room and curiosity got the better of her. She looked more closely at the crowd—all men. She assumed it was a bucks' night, Kings Cross was a favourite site for bucks' parties, and Ellie thought it was just as well they didn't know about the reunion for St Barbara's Catholic School for Girls going on next door. That could have been a recipe for disaster.

As Ellie turned to go back inside she caught sight of a familiar face.

Dark crescent-shaped eyebrows above chocolate eyes, full lips and a square jaw darkened by a day's growth of beard. Long lean lines and firm muscles. Just the sight of him, ten paces away, was enough to start her pulse racing, and the sound of his voice when he said her name sent a shiver of longing through her.

'Ellie?'

Her voice was husky as she replied. 'Dr Leonardi.'

'Please,' he said as he came towards her, bringing that strange humming sensation with him, 'my name is James. When you call me "Dr Leonardi" it makes me feel ancient.'

He'd closed the distance between them to a few inches, and they were separated only by the iron railing and surrounded by the humming bubble. She smiled up at him, her spirits buoyed by his presence. 'James.'

'What are you doing here?' he asked.

Ellie inclined her head towards the room behind her. 'A school reunion.'

'Are you having a good night?'

It just got ten times better, Ellie thought before she remembered her new list—no doctors allowed. She shrugged. 'It's been okay.'

James looked back over his shoulder. 'Co-ed school?'

'Catholic girls,' she said with a hint of a smile.

'Really?' He grinned at her and his chocolate eyes gleamed. 'I think you should go back inside and lock the doors before my lot find out who's in there.' He leant over the balcony for a better view into the function room and Ellie's face was almost nestled into the curve of his neck. He still smelt like limes.

Chocolate eyes and lime-scented skin—he was delicious.

He was leaning over her. She couldn't move. His scent had her mesmerised. She closed her eyes, blocking out the curve of his neck, the firm line of his jaw, the soft swell of his lips, but it didn't eliminate his smell. With her eyes closed her imagination kicked into overdrive. She could imagine how he would taste—like the rim of a tequila glass, lime with a dash of salt. She licked her lips, disappointed to find that the cheap champagne she'd been drinking tasted nothing like her imagination.

'Are you all right?' James' breath was warm on her cheek.

Her eyes snapped open. 'Yes, I'm fine,' she said as she tried to remember the thread of their conversation. She looked across to James's side of the balcony. *My lot*, he'd said. 'You're on a bucks' night?'

He nodded. 'I'm the best man and it's only fair to warn you that not all of my friends can be trusted.' He was still smiling, the curve of his lips widening to reveal even, white teeth.

'Don't worry.' She smiled in return. It seemed his smile had the power to elicit a response from her every time. 'Most of the girls can handle themselves and, besides, the nuns have all left and the boyfriends have just arrived.'

'Nuns? Seriously?' he asked as he stepped casually over the railing and sat on it with his feet on her side of the balcony. He appeared completely at ease but his proximity was making her tremble. He was close enough to touch yet there was space between them. He wasn't crowding her but she was extremely conscious that he was *there*. That's all. She was just supremely aware of the fact he was there.

She needed to step back, to put some distance between them, before she could answer. She nodded. 'They still exist, you know. Not all the teachers were nuns but the girls were like family to them, especially the ones who boarded. We spent a lot of time with them.'

'You were a boarder?' he asked. When she nodded he asked a second question. 'Where is your family from?'

'Goulburn.' Ellie divulged the name of the country town where she'd spent the first thirteen years of her life.

'I've been to Goulburn a few times on the way to the snow. Do you ski?'

'Not any more.' As soon as the words were out of her mouth she wanted to take them back. She could see the quizzical expression on James's face and she willed him not to ask the question she could see waiting in his eyes. She kept her focus on the activity on Darlinghurst Road. The Cross was starting to get busy now and it was easier to concentrate if she avoided looking into James's eyes. Somehow, the Cross, in all its seediness, was less dangerous. She chose to change the topic, hoping to distract him. 'So tell me, who's getting married?'

'One of my mates from uni.'

'Will you be next? Is that why you're the best

man?' In her imagination, James was single and this was the perfect opportunity to find out if she was right.

'No.' He shook his head. 'We've been friends since for ever, that's why I got the gig. Marriage isn't for me.'

'Why not?'

'One in three marriages ends in divorce.'

Ellie shrugged. 'The odds are still in your favour of it lasting the distance, though.'

'I'm not sure I believe in people's ability to commit to something of that magnitude. "Forsaking all others till death do us part" seems to be more than most people can handle. The expectations are very high, aren't they?'

She frowned. 'Your view makes you a bit of a strange choice for best man, wouldn't you say?'

'People are still going to get married, no matter what I think,' he replied. 'And Pete and Karen have been together since we started uni. What else are they going to do?

'You don't sound that thrilled for them.'

'I think they're settling.'

'Settling?'

He nodded. 'I get the feeling they think this is as good as it gets. It's almost as if they can't be bothered to search for something better.'

'Maybe it *is* as good as it gets.'

He shrugged. 'Possibly, but I would want fireworks and passion.'

Yes, you would, Ellie thought. It emanated from every pore in his body and he wouldn't be satisfied if that passion wasn't returned.

'Maybe they had that passion in the beginning,' she argued.

'Maybe they did but doesn't that make it worse, to think it's gone, that their best years are behind them? What's the point in getting married now, committing your life to one person, when you've had your best years?'

She wasn't convinced. 'Who's to say they've had their best years? They've got all that shared history and now they'll have a future too. If they've already been together for years I reckon they've got a pretty good chance.'

He was nodding his head. 'I guess they're one of those couples who reckon they'll make it,' he agreed.

Ellie smiled. 'I would say most couples who are planning on saying "I do" would tell you they thought they'd last the distance if you asked them. Otherwise why get married?'

'My point exactly.'

His smug tone made her laugh. 'I'm not agreeing with you,' she said. 'I'm saying that most people who get married believe their marriage will last.'

'Well, I hope you're right, for Pete and Karen's sake. You obviously have a less jaded view of marriage than I do. You believe in the whole happy-ever-after thing?'

She looked over the railing, turning her attention back to the action in the Cross, as she thought about her answer. Despite her many short-lived romances, including her most recent tumultuous break-up with a liar and a cheat, she did still believe in a happy ending. And for her, that included marriage. 'Yeah, I do. I'm still young and hopeful, not old and cynical like you.'

He laughed, a rich, deep laugh that drew Ellie's attention back to him. The tone of his laugh perfectly matched the dark intensity of his eyes. 'I'm not old and cynical,' he countered, 'I just want to keep my options open. Marriage doesn't allow for that.'

She was wondering if she could quiz him for more information when the sound of raised voices interrupted her train of thought. Two guys were being evicted from the pub across the road. They must have started a fight inside the pub and they showed no signs of giving up now they were outside. The two men, one in a leather jacket the other in a T-shirt, were throwing punches at each other and mostly missing. The guy in the jacket must have decided that tactic wasn't working and somehow he managed to get the other guy in a headlock.

Ellie watched horrified as the trapped man thrashed and kicked. 'Why doesn't someone do something?' There was nothing she and James could do from their first-floor vantage point and she wasn't about to try to break up a brawl between two men who, she assumed, had been drinking heavily. She didn't really expect any other passer-by to either but surely the security guards could do something? But the security guards had clearly abdicated responsibility now that they were off their premises.

'The police won't be far away.'

Ellie looked up and down Darlinghurst Road but couldn't see any sign of the blue uniforms. She wondered if she should phone 000 but then realised that James was right. This strip was usually heavily policed and they wouldn't be far away. If someone made a phone call every time there was a fight on Darlinghurst Road the phone lines would be permanently jammed. People were crossing the street, skirting the fight. No one wanted to get involved.

A girl came running out of the pub, yelling loudly, and Ellie's attention was pulled back to the action. The girl was very thin and dressed all in black, which accentuated her small frame. Ellie wondered what she was yelling about but without stopping to take a breath the girl leapt onto the back of the guy who was still trying to choke his opponent. Ellie couldn't believe what she was seeing. This girl, who couldn't weigh more than fifty kilograms, was pulling on the leather jacket of one man, trying to break up the fight. She had no chance as both men would easily weigh twice as much as her.

While keeping one arm around the throat of his opponent, the guy in the leather jacket reached behind him, grabbed the girl and flung her to the ground as easily as a cow swatted a fly with its tail. The girl tumbled through the air and her head collided with a metal street bench. Ellie's hand flew to her mouth. The girl was sprawled on the ground. She waited for someone to notice and go to her aid but people were still crossing the street to avoid the fracas and everyone seemed oblivious to the girl and her predicament. The fight was still in progress but the guy in the T-shirt had managed to get free of the headlock. Maybe the girl had provided just enough distraction to let him break free, but even he was more intent on attacking his opponent than helping the girl who had tried to help him. She still hadn't moved. Ellie waited for the girl to sit up. Nothing.

'She's not moving,' Ellie said to James, turning to look at him as she spoke.

But James was gone. He was running across

the balcony to the opposite corner. Ellie frowned. Where was he going?

He reached the edge of the balcony and Ellie saw him stretch over the side. There was a metal ladder fixed to the wall beside the balcony. She recognised it as an old fire escape. James knocked the ladder loose and Ellie heard the screech of stiff metal as the ladder extended. Ten seconds later he was down at street level.

Ellie finally processed the scene and followed in James's wake. The metal of the ladder was cold and rusty under her hands and she was a little slower than he had been thanks to her high heels, but at least she was wearing trousers. By the time she reached ground level James was kneeling beside the girl.

Ellie ran across the street, feeling about as graceful as a newborn giraffe in her high heels. The police had finally arrived but they were busy with the brawlers. They had managed to stop the fight and the two men were being hand-cuffed. The guy in the T-shirt, which was now hanging together by a few threads, had a bloody nose but somehow he'd managed to give the guy in leather a cut above his eye. Both injuries were bleeding profusely.

Ellie knelt beside James. She couldn't be sure but she guessed less than a minute had passed since the girl had hit her head. The girl's face was covered in blood from the gash beside her temple, it had run down the side of her face and was dripping from the end of her nose. James' fingers were on the girl's neck, feeling for a pulse.

'Is she alive?' she asked.

James looked around and he seemed almost surprised to see her. 'I can feel a pulse but she's not breathing. Get the cops to call an ambulance,' he said as he used his shirt to wipe the blood from around the girl's nose and mouth. Ellie knew he was preparing to breathe for the girl. She quickly grabbed a tissue from her handbag, it was the only precaution she could provide him with, before he tilted the girl's head back and started breathing air into her lungs.

There was nothing else for Ellie to do so she went and confirmed that an ambulance had been called, and according to the police it was on its way and she hoped James hadn't been foolish by starting resuscitation yet she knew he had no other option. As a doctor he had sworn on oath to do no harm and that meant attempting to save a life if he could with no regard for his own. She returned to his side. 'The paramedics are on the way,' she said.

As she spoke she heard the girl breathe in on her own. James quickly sat back and turned the girl onto her side, narrowly escaping a stream of vomit that spilled from her.

'Don't move.' James had one hand on the girl's shoulder, keeping her in position. 'You've been in an accident, you hit your head and you need to be checked over.' The ambulance pulled alongside the kerb and the paramedics climbed out. Even though James was preventing the girl from sitting up, Ellie could see that her hands were moving so it didn't look as though she'd sustained any serious injury. She'd been lucky. Lucky too that James had been on the scene.

Ellie sat on the metal bench that had played a part in the drama and waited while James handed the girl over to the paramedics. She didn't know what else to do. She couldn't walk away but it felt strange waiting for James, as though they were in this together.

The two pugilists had been bundled into the back of two police vans. The cops were keeping them separated and under surveillance, obviously taking no chances, while the pub's security guards gave their version of the night's events. Next James had to give his details to the police and then he was free to go. Ellie stood and approached him when he'd finished. She put one hand on his arm and the warmth of his skin seeping into her fingers comforted her and unsettled her at the same time. She felt both safe and vulnerable. An odd sensation until she worked out that he affected her head and her body in different ways. Her head said he was a good person, honest and trustworthy. That was the safe part. It was her own body and her reaction to him that she couldn't trust.

'Are you okay?' she asked.

'Yeah.'

The bottom of his shirt was bloodstained from where he'd wiped the girl's face and there was a bloody handprint down the side where he must have wiped his own hand at some point. His forehead was wet with perspiration. Ellie could smell the faint metallic scent of blood but the smell of limes was still quite strong and there was now a definite saltiness to James's scent as well. Despite his dishevelled state, he still smelt fantastic.

'That was quite a performance, very James Bond, racing to the rescue down the fire escape,' she said.

'Oh God, James Bond?' He lifted his hands and rubbed his face, smearing his forehead with dirt and blood. 'I must have looked like a complete idiot.' Despite the grime he still looked striking. The dirt streaked his cheekbones, emphasising their sharp angles, and his teeth appeared even whiter in contrast to the dark smudges of grime.

Ellie shook her head. 'No. It was all rather impressive, to be honest. You saved that girl's life. She was lucky you were around.'

'I guess so,' he said modestly. 'I just hope she feels better tomorrow.' He'd been half turned away from her but now he turned to face her squarely, his chocolate eyes dark in his face. 'What shall we do now?'

'What do you mean?' Ellie asked.

'Are you going back to your party?'

Ellie looked up at the balcony. It was almost impossible to believe she'd started the night up there. She couldn't imagine going back now. She shook her head. 'I think I might head home. I've had enough excitement for one day.'

'Are you driving?'

'No,' she shook her head. 'I'll get a taxi.' There was no point in explaining she didn't have a car.

'I have my car, I needed to stay sober and responsible tonight. Let me take you home.'

'What about your friends?' she asked. As much as she would love a lift home, she didn't want him to feel obliged to help her.

James checked his watch. 'They'll be heading downstairs to the basement soon. I doubt they'll even notice I'm missing. Besides, I'm more than happy to skip that part.'

Ellie knew the basement housed a strip club, or, as the business owners phrased it, a 'gentlemen's club'. 'That's going to a lot of trouble for you. It's fine really, I'll catch a cab.' She gave him one last chance to change his mind.

'Please. I'd feel much happier if I drove you. I don't like the idea of you getting a cab on your own, not from the Cross. I'll drive you home and come back. Are you near the hospital?'

She nodded.

'That's settled, then. It'll be half an hour, easy.'

He took her hand and led her across the road. His touch startled her and set her pulse racing. She felt as though there was an invisible line running from her palm straight to her heart and the touch of James's hand had sent the silent hum that normally surrounded them directly through her veins. Her lips were dry and her heart was hammering in her chest yet he was behaving as if it was nothing unusual, as it if were something they did every day. But the familiarity, while not unpleasant, surprised her.

She expected him to let go of her hand once they reached the opposite footpath but he didn't. His hand felt warm and strong and gave her something to focus on instead of thinking about the drama she'd just witnessed. The drama he had single-handedly sorted.

He kept hold of her hand until they reached the parking garage and she concentrated on using his touch to make her feel safe as she tried to block out the other more primal sensations she was experiencing.

He only let go of her when he needed to dig his car keys out of his pocket, using them to unlock a black Jeep. His car wasn't old and neither was it new but, more importantly, there were no baby seats in the back or anything else to indicate that he might have a family stashed away somewhere. He'd said he wasn't going to get married but he didn't say he hadn't already been married, and either way he could still have children. Not that it should matter, she told herself. Even if smouldering, wild and dark hadn't been cut from her list, doctors had.

He saw her checking out the car. The back seat was strewn with clothes and, understandably, he misunderstood her interest. 'I've been living out of my car a bit for the past couple of weeks,' he explained.

'Why?'

'I live on the North Shore,' he explained. 'It's a bit of a trek in the traffic from the hospital across the harbour to my place depending on what shifts I pull so sometimes it's easier just to stay in one of the on-call rooms.'

No wife, no baby seats and happy not to go home every night—he was definitely single.

Not that it mattered, she reminded herself again, it was of no consequence to her. She wasn't ever going to date another doctor, even ones who smelt as delicious as he did and had chocolate eyes that could melt a girl's heart.

He held the door open for her before circling the car and climbing in to his seat. The small, enclosed confines of the car accentuated the tension in the air that constantly seemed to surround him. She could feel it throbbing around her and the air was filled with the aroma of limes. His smell.

Maybe getting a lift was a bad idea.

She shifted a little in her seat and crossed her arms over her chest, trying vainly to distance herself.

'Are you cold?' He reached for the controls for the heater.

'No.' She forced herself to relax. She couldn't very well tell him she needed to keep her arms folded to stop herself from reaching over to touch him. She couldn't tell him how his lime scent and the buzz she got just from being near him was enough to drive her crazy with desire. How she was tempted to reach over and taste him, to run her fingers through his hair and stretch one hand out to feel if his thighs were as strong as they looked under the denim of his jeans. She couldn't tell him any of that so she chatted about nothing as she directed him to the house on Hill Street.

'Did you want to come in and use the bathroom?' she asked as he pulled to a stop out the front. 'You've got dirt and blood all over you.'

He flipped the sun visor down and had a very brief glance at his face in the mirror on the reverse side. 'Might not be a bad idea, thanks.' He reached behind the seat and picked up a couple of T-shirts, choosing one and discarding the other. 'I should change my top too, I guess.'

He hopped out of the car and pulled his bloodied shirt over his head, not bothering to undo the buttons, and tossed it into the back seat. He was standing in the street, half-naked, and Ellie knew she should look away. She knew she was staring but her eyes were glued to the scene. It was a repeat of the beach volleyball episode, a shirtless James, tanned and muscled. But tonight was better because she was closer. His chest was smooth, brown and virtually hairless and she could see his abdominal muscles ripple as he ducked his head into the T-shirt and tugged it down. His lean physique reminded her of a sleek cat, more black panther than lion, though, despite his name.

She was finding it hard to breathe. He had literally taken her breath away.

'One of the benefits of keeping my wardrobe in my car,' he said with a grin as his head emerged from his shirt.

She smiled back, hoping she wasn't grinning like a fool, before she led the way into her house. She found a clean towel and showed him to the bathroom.

'Can I get you something to drink before you go?' she asked when he emerged. She hoped she sounded like she was offering out of politeness and not as though she was propositioning him.

'Thanks, but I'd better get back to the bucks' night just to make sure everything is under control. Can I take a rain-check?' He stopped beside her and handed her the towel he'd used. 'Would you go out for a drink with me some other time? Somewhere a bit more civilised than the Cross?'

He was standing just inches from her. The faint metallic scent of blood had been washed from his skin and his fresh, lime scent filled her head once more. His offer was tempting, very tempting. She met his gaze. His dark eyes were watching her intently and she very nearly said yes before she remembered her list.

'I'm sorry, I can't.'

'Can't? Or won't?'

'Both.'

'Any particular reason?' he asked.

'I don't date people from work.'

A frown creased his forehead, his brown eyes puzzled. 'Why not?'

'It's complicated.'

'I promise I can keep it simple. You, me, a bar somewhere.' He smiled at her and replaced his frown with a wink.

It did sound simple. And tempting. What could be the harm in that?

But she'd been burned before. It really was too bad because he was truly divine.

'Let me know if you change your mind,' he said into her silence. His voice was just a breath in her ear and then he was gone. He moved easily, quietly and suddenly there was nothing except for a faint, lingering trace of lime to suggest he'd even been in her house.

But Ellie had the image of him in her head. How he'd run lightly across the balcony, his lithe frame moving quickly, dropping down the fire-escape ladder, kneeling over the girl on the pavement. How the touch of his hand had warmed her from the outside while his smile had warmed her from the inside.

James was hot. He made her insides melt and he smelt like her favourite things, but he wasn't for her. That was all there was to it. She'd have to look elsewhere.

She should go to bed and forget all about James Leonardi, but going to bed wasn't the answer. All she did was revisit all the things she knew about him. The way his hair curled at his temples, the creases that appeared at the corners of his eyes when he smiled and the warmth of his hand on her skin. The ripple of his abdominals when he'd changed his shirt and the beautiful golden tone of his skin.

Quite simply, he was gorgeous.

But, despite all that, he was still off-limits.

CHAPTER FOUR

FOR two days he thought she'd disappeared, like Cinderella after the ball, and he couldn't stop thinking about her. Was she rostered off or was she on nights? Why hadn't he thought to ask about her shifts?

Because he wasn't thinking straight, that's why.

And the more time that passed, the more he thought about her. About the golden glow that surrounded her and seemed to warm everything and everyone around her. It had wrapped itself around him and pulled him to her, drawing him in close. He'd had to drag himself away to go back to the bucks' party on Saturday night and it hadn't been easy. If he hadn't been Pete's best man he would probably have ditched his mates but duty had called.

He'd wanted to stay with Ellie and he'd wanted

to kiss her. But he'd fought the urge. He couldn't take that liberty, especially not while she was refusing to go on a date with him. But he was sure that she'd been tempted to say yes. He was certain she'd been wavering. It wasn't possible that he was the only one who felt the chemistry between them. It was too strong to be one-sided.

He found it hard to believe that just two weeks earlier he'd talked himself out of asking her on a date. Despite Mavis's advice he'd gone with the sensible option, sticking to his bachelor ways, knowing he was busy concentrating on his career. Combining his career with a relationship hadn't worked out so well for him before but the minute he was alone with Ellie he'd forgotten all about being sensible. All he could think of was her and how she made him feel. He wanted to suffuse himself in her golden glow, he wanted to let it wrap itself around them both, cocooning them away from the world. She made him forget all his past failings. She made him believe any-thing was possible and he wouldn't rest until he worked out how to convince her to go out with him. But first he had to work out what shift she was on.

He finally remembered the nurses' roster that was pinned to the board on the orthopaedic ward. He checked it and was pleased to find that Ellie was on for an early shift the following day. He'd be in Theatre in the morning but he'd make sure he caught up with her at some stage.

The morning dragged, the cases on the operating list were routine, boring even, and James found himself, on more than one occasion, with one eye on the clock, waiting for the end of theatre. The only thing that helped to pass the time was quizzing people about Ellie. Did she date? What did she like to do? What could anyone tell him?

Rob didn't participate in the conversation and James could only assume it was because he had nothing to contribute. He seemed to be in another one of his moods, which James chose to ignore. Despite his infatuation with Ellie he was able to focus on the job while he was in Theatre so he knew Rob couldn't have any issue with him.

He changed out of his dirty scrubs as quickly as possible at the end of the list and headed for the canteen, hoping to run into Ellie. The canteen was busy and he scanned the room as he waited for his salad roll and coffee. She was there, sitting with Charlotte, the ward physio, and there was a spare table beside them. With luck that table would still be free once he had his order.

He paid for his lunch and weaved his way through the throng towards Ellie, grateful the canteen was bustling as it made it look quite natural that he would cross the room, searching for one of the few vacant spots. He was within a few metres of the empty table when two orderlies claimed it. He stopped, his plans thwarted. There was a third vacant chair at the table but it would be most unusual for him to sit with other hospital employees, particularly non-medical staff. The doctors tended to sit together, no one seemed to expect anything else, and to do otherwise would no doubt make everyone feel uncomfortable. He'd have to search for a different table.

As he stood there, pondering his options, Charlotte spotted him and came to his rescue.

'Hi, Dr Leonardi, you're welcome to sit with us.'

He gratefully accepted her offer. 'Thank you.' He closed the distance between them and put his coffee on the table. 'I haven't seen you on the ward for a few days, Ellie. Have you been off?' he asked as he sat down.

Ellie shook her head, her blonde hair shining in the light. 'I had yesterday day off, but I've been on nights.'

Nights. Of course. Movement to his left caught James's attention. Someone had stopped beside their table and was pulling out the last remaining chair.

Ellie made the introductions as this stranger, very confidently in James's opinion, took a seat.

'James, Damien Clark is a physio, he works in Outpatients. Damien, this is James Leonardi, the new orthopod.'

Damien extended his hand. 'I've seen your name on some case notes, it's nice to put a face to a name,' he said as he shook James's hand.

'Welcome to Eastern Beaches.' He didn't wait for a response from James. He sat on the other side of Ellie and James noticed that he moved his chair a fraction closer to hers as he sat down. Was he another one of Ellie's admirers?

'Are you thinking any more positively about the movie today, Ellie, or is it still not your favourite?' Damien was asking.

'It's nowhere near my favourite,' Ellie replied.

They'd been to a movie together?

James saw how Damien looked at Ellie, desperate for her approval, wanting to please her, and he experienced a sudden, unexpected flash of jealousy. Had Ellie been on a date with Damien? He knew it was none of his business except she'd told him she didn't date people from work.

'In that case, we'll have to try again,' Damien was saying.

James moved his leg, just a fraction, enough to bring his knee into contact with Ellie's. The slight touch had the desired effect. He could feel the energy pulsing between them and it moved Ellie's attention away from Damien and his proposal. Ellie looked at him and he knew she could feel the heat too, he could see it in her eyes. The feeling of jealousy that had surged through him was replaced with one of satisfaction.

James knew he was being juvenile but he couldn't help it, he wasn't going to sit here and compete with Damien for Ellie's attention. Not unless he was going to win. And he knew he held the trump card. He and Ellie had a connection, a strong connection, and he wasn't going to let go easily.

Ellie pushed her chair back from the table, her gaze still locked with his. 'I'd better be heading back.'

She leant down to pick her handbag up from underneath the table and her hair brushed over his forearm. He quickly gathered up the remains of his lunch and stood too.

'I'll walk back with you,' he said. He wanted to walk away from this lunch victorious and the only way to do that was to make sure Ellie left with him and not Damien.

'I'll call you,' Damien said to Ellie. Whether Ellie noticed it or not, James knew that Damien recognised the competition and he was making sure James knew it too.

'You didn't enjoy the movie?' James asked as they walked together towards the lifts.

'Not particularly,' Ellie replied. 'It was supposed to be a romantic comedy but it wasn't very romantic nor was it particularly funny. The two lead characters had no spark.'

'You went with Damien?' He tried to keep his tone neutral but he wasn't sure how successful he was.

'And Charlotte and her fiancé,' Ellie replied as she pressed the button for the lift.

'And Damien works in Outpatients?'

'Yes.'

They stepped into the full lift and James saved his question, waiting until they got out again. He didn't want to have this conversation in front of a crowd.

'I thought you didn't date people from work?' he asked as the lift delivered them to the Orthopaedic ward.

'People from other departments don't count.'

'That's discrimination,' he said.

'Against who?'

'Me.'

Ellie laughed. 'Sorry, but that's my new rule.'

'Well, I'd like to go on record as saying that I think it's an extremely bad rule and I'd like to object to it.'

'You can object all you like but it makes no difference. Besides, I'd hardly call it a date.'

His response was a raised eyebrow.

'Going to the movies with a group of friends doesn't count,' she clarified.

'Does Damien know that?' he asked.

She shrugged. 'It wasn't ever a proper date.' Not in her mind anyway. Charlotte had bullied her into going to the movies. She'd been one of the few people who knew of her relationship with Rob and she'd been convinced it would do Ellie good to get out and meet someone new, someone who wasn't a doctor. Ellie had insisted that it should all be very casual and she'd only gone on the proviso that Charlotte and her fiancé came too. Charlotte thought she was helping to cheer Ellie up but Ellie had accepted for a different reason altogether, to distract her from her fantasies about James. Maybe Damien would suit her and maybe he'd get her mind off James, who was most unsuitable!

But of course it hadn't worked. There was no spark, no connection with Damien. She didn't get all warm and tingly when he looked at her. She didn't want to touch him, taste him, devour him the way she did James. No. The movie date hadn't done anything except show her that she could resist some men and remind her how she felt about James.

'So, by your admission, a date isn't a date if there are other people involved,' James said with a grin.

'Something like that.'

'So, a game of beach volleyball, two on two, wouldn't count?'

'Possibly not.'

'Good, because I need a partner on Sunday morning. Would you come and play with me?' He must have sensed her hesitation because he added clarification. 'It's not a date, we'll be in a public place with lots of other people.'

It wasn't the where or when that bothered her,

it was the 'what'. 'Beach volleyball?' she queried. Ball sports were not her forte. 'Surely I'm too short?'

'You'll be fine. I'll cover for you.'

'Wouldn't you rather get someone else to partner you? Someone taller? Someone with better hand-eye co-ordination than me?'

James shook his head. 'I want you.'

She had no retort for that. *He wanted her!* A girl would have to be crazy to pass up the invitation now.

She'd sworn not to date another orthopod but if James was insisting this wasn't a date she could choose to believe him. Surely she could trust herself not to fall under his spell.

But she knew she wasn't immune to his charm when they were on the ward, she wasn't immune to his charm when they were in his car, and she didn't imagine she'd be immune on the beach, in broad daylight, surrounded by crowds. The more time she spent with him, the harder it was going to be to resist the attraction.

She shouldn't accept his invitation. It was madness. But she didn't have enough willpower to refuse.

'Okay, I just hope you know what you're doing 'cos I'll tell you now, I have no idea.' If James thought she was just talking about beach volleyball that was fine by her, but her comment covered a multitude of situations.

The morning sun was warm on her skin as she made her way down to the beach but it was nothing compared to the warmth that flooded through her when she saw James waiting for her. He crossed the beach, his movements effortless even through the soft, dry sand, and met her as she descended the steps. The air around them hummed as she was enveloped in his lime scent. He reached for her hands and the humming travelled through her body. She was convinced she could feel every individual nerve ending pulsing as it responded to his touch.

He leant forward and greeted her with a kiss on each cheek. His gesture took her by surprise. Unlike after the Kings Cross incident, when she'd half expected him to kiss her and he hadn't, this kiss was completely unforeseen and therefore all the more exciting. Her skin tingled where his lips met her cheeks but he was behaving as if his greeting was nothing unusual so she attempted to follow his lead.

'Good morning, I'm glad you could make it. Come.' He wrapped one arm around her shoulders and guided her to the courts marked in the sand. His arm was warm across her bare skin and she fought hard to concentrate on getting her feet to move forward. It was difficult to focus on anything else while he was touching her.

She'd spent ages choosing her outfit and now she wished she'd chosen something that covered her up a bit more. Despite there being a limited number of outfits that were suitable for a game of beach volleyball she'd managed to change her clothes half a dozen times before settling on a blue sports singlet and short white shorts. Bikinis were out, she wasn't prepared for the stress of worrying about which bits of her were spilling out of a pair of bathers, and she was too short to wear board shorts. Jogging clothes were the most flattering, she'd decided.

But slightly more protection might have been wise. It wasn't the sun she needed protection from, she'd applied plenty of sunscreen, but if James was going to keep touching her exposed skin there was no way she was going to be able to concentrate on a game of volleyball. She didn't have a clue how to play the game anyway and she knew James was going to be a huge distraction, albeit a very pleasant one.

Several people were already warming up, hitting the ball back and forth over the net. It didn't look too difficult. Normally, she would have declined the invitation, ball sports were not her thing, but it hadn't taken much for James to persuade her. Perhaps she could do this.

'Let me teach you some of the shots,' he said as he stripped off his shirt and tossed it onto a towel that was lying beside the beach wall. His skin was a smooth golden brown, his shoulders nicely square and his abdominal muscles rippled. A shirtless James was a sight she didn't think she could ever grow tired of. He took her beach bag from her as she stood admiring the view and put it with his things. If he noticed her fixation he didn't comment. 'It's a pretty easy game, there aren't too many things you need to know before you can make a decent go of it. You need to know a throw, a dig, a spike and a serve.'

'That's all?' That sounded like an awful lot!

'Here.' He picked up a ball that was lying on the sand and tossed it to her. To her relief, she caught it. 'First, the throw. Generally you try to use this when you receive a serve, it takes the pace off the ball and lets the next person set up a dig.'

Her expression must have been one of total confusion. 'Don't worry, it's not hard. Throw the ball to me, I'll show you.'

She threw him the ball, a flat pass aimed at his chest, just like she remembered learning in netball. James caught it.

'Good throw but in volleyball you do it like this.' He lofted the ball into the air and as it came down towards him he lifted his arms above his head pushing the ball back up into the air. 'There, that's all there is to it.'

Ellie had no idea what he was talking about.

She hadn't seen what he'd done, her attention had been distracted by his arm movements and the flow-on effect it had had on the muscles of his back and shoulders. 'Can you show me again?'

He repeated the action and this time she forced herself to concentrate. She watched the ball, keeping her focus on the inanimate object.

'Your turn,' he said as he looped the ball to her.

Ellie reached up for it, squinting into the sun. The ball collided with her fingers but instead of flying back up into the air, as it had done for James, it stopped dead and fell to the ground.

'You need to keep your elbows bent and straighten them as you push the ball up,' James explained. He took a step to her side and held her elbows, lifting them up in line with her ears, with her hands above her head. 'Start here and when the ball lands on your fingers then straighten your elbows. You want to push the ball back to me. If you throw, I'll dig.'

'You know I'm not understanding a word you're saying, don't you?' Ellie laughed. *And*

I can't concentrate when you're touching me, she wanted to add. She didn't give two hoots about volleyball, all she wanted was for James to run his hands back down her arms and from there to her waist. If she closed her eyes she could imagine exactly how it would feel. How he would feel.

'Trust me, it's not hard.'

'Are you sure you don't want to choose a different partner while you've still got time?'

'Positive. I'm going to teach you how to dig now.' He let go of her elbows and she could breathe again but her skin ached for his touch. 'You've got to use a different grip for this,' he said as he took hold of her hands. 'You have to interlock your fingers…' he threaded her fingers together '…palms facing each other…' he closed her hands '…and make a flat surface from your thumbs to your wrists…' He ran his fingers along her thumbs and up to her wrists. 'You want to hit the ball here,' he said as he circled a spot on her wrist.

Her skin was on fire, every nerve ending in her wrist, hand and fingers was quivering and she was surprised that she could see no visible shaking. 'Still no idea what you're saying.' She laughed. She knew she didn't have a hope in hell of getting the ball to do anything when her hands felt as though they didn't belong to her.

'Give it a shot.' James threw the ball to himself and used the 'throw' to pass it to her.

Somehow she managed to hit the ball but it went sailing backwards over her head. She collapsed in a fit of giggles. 'I'm guessing it wasn't supposed to go in that direction.'

'No.' He was laughing, with her she hoped, not at her, but at least he didn't look ready to trade her for someone else just yet.

'I thought you said this was an easy game.'

'It is. Let me show you.' He came and stood behind her this time. 'You need to keep your elbows straight for this shot.' He wrapped his arms around hers, laying them along the outside of hers as he straightened her elbows. His hips were pressing into her bottom and he used his legs to pull her down into a slight squat. 'Get yourself behind the ball and keep your elbows straight. Angle your arms down here…' he pulled her hands down to a forty-five-degree angle to the sand '…so that when the ball hits your wrists you're aiming it up and forward. Straighten your knees to get the power behind the ball.' He tightened his arms around her and pulled her up into a standing position. 'You need to master the "dig" because you're probably not tall enough for the "spike".'

She still had absolutely no idea what he was talking about, but she could feel his thigh muscles pushing against her buttocks, guiding her into position. Even through a couple of layers of clothing the sensation was highly charged. She didn't think she'd ever get the hang of the actual game but the lessons sure were enjoyable.

'Try again.' He let go of her arms and picked the ball up from the sand.

This time she managed to get the ball to travel forward. A huge achievement.

'Well done! Now a serve and that's it. Normally we aim for the back left corner of our opponent's court but anything over the net will be good.'

'Don't be rude! I'm sure I can manage that.'

At least she knew what a serve was supposed to look like, that was fairly obvious from other games of beach volleyball that she'd walked past. She picked up the ball, went to stand behind the base line and popped the ball over the net just as James had told her to. 'I did it!'

'All right!' James grinned and high-fived her and Ellie felt invincible. 'Let's find someone to have a practice against.'

As she expected, a game situation was a little different. It was a lot faster and she didn't have James's hands around her to guide her. The ball went flying in all directions, occasionally making it over the net and landing in their opponents' court, but to his credit James just laughed and continued to encourage her, even when she served the ball straight into the back of his head.

'I'm so sorry. Are you okay?'

'Yes, I'm fine.' He laughed. 'I just wasn't expecting that one! I'll be ready next time.'

They persevered for an hour or so before James declared it was time to call it quits. 'I think we've lost by as much as we can. I reckon we should call it a day and go for a swim.'

Ellie hadn't worn bathers and despite the sun-shine she knew the water would be cold. 'Too cold for me,' she said as she pulled her drink bottle out of her bag, 'but you go ahead.' She picked up their towels and carried them down to the water's edge.

James jogged into the water and dived through the waves. He swam several strokes out to sea before turning and swimming back to shore. He came out of the water, wet and glistening, and collapsed onto his towel beside her. The cool water had hardened his nipples and Ellie fought to keep her eyes fixed on the waves. She could feel the difference in their body heat now. He was sitting very close to her and the contrast between the coolness of his skin and the warmth of hers was palpable. She could smell him too, limes mingled with the salty tang of the ocean. A fresh, clean scent that would always make her think of him.

'Have you enjoyed our "non-date"?' he asked.

'I actually have,' she admitted. Despite the fact that she'd failed spectacularly at beach volleyball, she'd had one of the best mornings ever. 'Thank you.'

'My pleasure,' he said. He smiled at her and even though she hadn't thought the day could get any better, once again the power of his smile made everything seem just that little bit more special.

In James's opinion yesterday's 'non-date' had worked perfectly. He knew Ellie had enjoyed it and now it was time to up the ante. He was going to get her to agree to a proper date. He was going to get past her obstacles and over her objections. He picked up the phone in the doctors' lounge and dialled the extension for the nurses' station.

Ellie answered the ward phone, surprised to hear James's voice. Even from afar his voice sent her pulse racing.

'Ellie!' He sounded pleased she'd answered. 'I have a favour to ask. I've got a case study to present and I thought I might use Dylan Harris as he's got some interesting psychological aspects. Would you mind bringing me his case notes?'

If it had been any of the other doctors she would have told them she was too busy and they'd have to get the notes themself. But because it was James she was willing to do it. Did that make her a hypocrite? She knew it did but she didn't care. After their 'non-date' the attraction she felt was becoming harder to resist, the invisible link she could feel between them pulled her to him at every opportunity and it was getting stronger.

She found Dylan's file and carried it down the corridor to the doctors' lounge. James was waiting just inside the door and he held it open for her as she stepped into the room. She took a few steps forward, aware that James was close behind her. She stopped beside a small couch and turned and handed him the file. He dropped the notes onto the couch, making no pretence of looking at them.

Ellie looked around. Except for them the lounge was empty. It was a generously sized room but Ellie was only aware of how close James was standing. He hadn't stepped away from her and she hadn't moved. She didn't think she could. She was held motionless by their energy field, that invisible bubble. She waited for him to speak, somehow knowing he would, knowing he had something to say.

'The movie date you went on with Damien...'

'Mmm.' She heard his words but was grateful he hadn't formed a question because she didn't think she could articulate an answer while he was standing so close. She knew she should remind him that it hadn't been a proper date but her brain couldn't think beyond the basic senses. She could smell him, his now-familiar lime scent. She could hear him, his deep, warm, rich voice. She wanted to touch him, to feel his smooth olive skin and taste him. She could imagine how his lips would taste. It was as though all her functions had shut down except for the basics. She couldn't formulate anything sensible.

'Was it as much fun as our game of beach volleyball?'

She shook her head. 'It was nice.' Three words. That was all she could manage and even they were a struggle.

'Nice?' he queried. 'How about our non-date, how would you describe that?'

Now she was definitely lost for words. How did you tell someone your head was still spinning from the memory of the touch of his hand on her skin? How did you describe the way her heart raced when his arms wrapped around her as he taught her the game?

'Better than nice?' he suggested when no reply came from her.

She nodded.

'Would you go out on a proper date with Damien, do you think?'

This time she shook her head.

'How about with me? Has our non-date changed your mind about me at all?'

'Why would it have?' she asked, surprised to find she was able to tease him.

'Because of this.' He reached out and ran his hand along her arm. He started at her elbow, where her arm emerged from her short-sleeved shirt. His fingers burned over her skin until he reached her wrist. He turned her hand over and ran his thumb over her palm and a ripple of desire surged through her belly. The air around them buzzed. 'You feel it too, don't you?' She could feel a pulse in her throat throbbing, her heart was racing and her breaths were short and shallow. 'And I know you couldn't have felt that with Damien because there's no way on earth you could describe this as "nice". This is something else. This is chemistry. Pure and simple.'

She took a deep breath, inhaling his subtle lime scent, holding it in her chest.

'When he held your hand in the movies you didn't forget to breathe, did you?'

She couldn't remember Damien holding her hand but she knew James was right. It wouldn't have had the same effect. It wouldn't have come close. And he was right about her not breathing too. She couldn't breathe but she didn't feel as though she needed to. James's touch was all she needed.

Her legs felt like jelly. She didn't think she could support her own weight. James moved his hands to her hips, holding her up, supporting her. She looked up at him, into the depths of his chocolate eyes, as he moved towards her.

'And when his knee brushed against your thigh it didn't make you quiver with anticipation.' His voice was a whisper. His words a statement. He slid one hand down her thigh and the heat of it burned through the fabric of her trousers. She trembled, grateful she was pressed up against the back of the couch, sandwiched between the furniture and James's hips. She couldn't move. She didn't want to move. His face was mere inches from hers.

'And when he leant towards you, did you find yourself leaning in just a little bit closer?' He lifted one hand, pressing his fingertips to the pulse that was throbbing in her neck as his thumb brushed over her lips. Another ripple of desire ran through her. Automatically she parted her lips, her tongue darting out to lick them. She saw James's gaze follow the movement, she could see her own desire reflected in his eyes and heard him moan as he bent his head towards her, closing the gap. His chest pressed against hers as his head came down and she felt her nipples harden in response. His breath was warm on her mouth. And then his lips were on hers. Firm and warm, and this time it was her moaning.

CHAPTER FIVE

His lips tasted of salt, his mouth of coffee. His hand slid up her back, crushing her to him. His tongue was inside her mouth, exploring, as his hands moved over her body. His fingers brushed over one breast, sending a spark of desire through her, so intense it made her gasp. James stopped kissing her, pulling away, and she knew he was checking that she was okay. His eyes searched her face.

She was fine. She smiled and she could see passion flare in his eyes. There was fire in their dark depths. She'd thought his eyes were brown but now they looked black, as black as coal, and she knew how coal could burn.

'What are we doing?' She sounded out of breath. She was out of breath.

'Something I've wanted to do since the first day I saw you.' His hands were firm against her arms, holding her to him as if he were afraid she might leave. But there was nowhere she wanted to go.

Until she remembered where they were.

'What if someone walks in?' she said in a panic. She didn't think her heart could beat any faster but the idea that someone could walk into the doctors' lounge at any moment and find them there, together, scared her.

'I locked the door behind us.'

That surprised her. He must have thought this through and it made her wonder how many times he'd been in this situation. Obviously more times than her! 'You were that confident I'd let you kiss me?'

'It pays to be prepared.' He grinned at her, not at all embarrassed. His eyes shone and desire flared in her again. 'But you're free to leave if you wish.' He stepped to one side. Ellie could easily step around him and make her escape but she made no such move. Instead she reached out to him, pulling him back to her. She had one hand on his back and she could feel the muscles flex under her fingers as he stepped towards her.

She wound her other hand through his thick, dark hair and pulled his head down to her again. He didn't resist as she kissed him.

Ellie forgot about her list. About her pledge not to date another doctor. This wasn't a date. This was a chemistry lesson. Just as James had said.

But chemistry had never been this much fun at school.

Eventually she came to her senses and remembered she was in the middle of her shift. She couldn't believe she'd forgotten all about work. 'I'd better get back on the ward.'

She wouldn't have thought she was the type of girl who sneaked off at work but, then, she'd never felt this undeniable attraction before. She'd never been this powerless, never had her body betray her mind to such a degree.

'So I take it you'll have that drink with me now?'

So much for not getting involved with another orthopaedic surgeon! She didn't have enough willpower to stay away from him. She knew that if he wanted her, he would have her and she'd go willingly. She couldn't fight this feeling. She nodded.

'Tonight?' he asked.

She tried to recall what she was doing after work. Damn. She and Jess had a class to go to.

'I can't tonight.'

'You're not going out with Damien, are you?'

Ellie was tempted to say yes just to hear what he'd say, but he looked so anxious that she took pity on him. 'No, I'm doing a course with a girl-friend.' She was rewarded with a wide smile that made her add. 'And we'll probably go to the Stat Bar for a drink afterwards. Around nine.'

James smile grew even wider. 'Nine?'

Ellie nodded.

'I'll see you later, then,' he said, before he leant forward and kissed her on the mouth.

She knew she had to get back to the ward, she couldn't stay hidden away in the doctors' lounge with James all day, as much as she wanted to, but it was all she could do to get her feet moving one at a time when he opened the door for her. He stuck his head out into the corridor, making sure it was clear, and Ellie hurried back to the ward, hoping no one had noticed her absence. She ducked into the staff toilet to check her appearance. Her lips felt swollen and her eyes were a bright, sparkling blue but she didn't think anyone else would notice anything amiss. She ran her fingers through her hair, repositioning her Alice band, and straightened her shirt before returning to her duties.

She floated through the rest of her shift on a little bubble of happiness and even Rob's mid-afternoon visit to the ward didn't dampen her spirits.

Ellie kept her commitment to Jess, accompanying her to the wine appreciation class they'd enrolled in, but she spent the entire evening with one eye on the clock wishing she could leave and hurry to the Stat Bar. It didn't help matters that Jess had chosen the class thinking it might be a good place to meet men who weren't doctors but there certainly wasn't a lot in the way of potential. They both struggled through the class as Ellie regaled Jess with a slightly edited version of the afternoon's events and after that it didn't take much effort from her to persuade Jess to call in to the Stat Bar to meet Ruby and Cort for a drink.

They'd only been at the bar a few minutes and were waiting for Ruby to arrive when Ellie felt the hair on the back of her neck rise, as if a warm breeze has brushed over her. She knew, before even seeing the look on Jess's face, that James was behind her.

'Hello, gorgeous.' He leant over her shoulder and his voice was soft in her ear as his breath warmed the nape of her neck. To hear him use such a familiar greeting in public both surprised and excited her.

His fingers were resting lightly on her upper arm and she was enveloped in his lime scent. She felt a rush of desire as the memory of the afternoon came flooding back with his touch. She turned in her chair and greeted him before introducing him to Jess.

'Can I buy you both a drink?' he asked.

'I'm fine, thanks,' Jess replied. 'Why don't you go with James, Ellie?' she suggested.

'Are you sure?'

'Yes, go.' Jess waved them away. 'I can see Ruby heading over now,' she said as she dismissed them both, guessing correctly that Ellie didn't want to share James.

Ellie didn't need to be asked twice. She stood and left with James.

Two steps into the bar she wished she'd stayed in her seat because sitting at a table, right in their path, was Rob with a woman Ellie didn't recognise. She was a brunette and Ellie assumed she was Rob's wife but, with Rob's track record, she wasn't about to jump to conclusions. But if she was Rob's wife, she wasn't at all what Ellie had pictured—she was tall and thin with long dark hair tied into a ponytail and a long face.

Rob stood to shake James's hand but ignored Ellie and made no attempt to introduce the woman he was with. James made the introductions himself as Rob sat down.

'I'm Penny, Rob's wife,' the woman responded to James's introduction.

Hearing her assumptions confirmed gave Ellie a moment of relief as she realised she'd been wondering what Rob's wife was like. She'd envisaged a glamorous English rose but the bitchy side of her was pleased to see that Penny was older and plainer than she'd imagined.

James was being far more gracious. 'I thought you must be,' he said. 'Welcome to Australia. How are you settling in?'

Ellie saw Penny glance at Rob as she answered, 'It will take a little bit of time to adjust but we're getting sorted.'

'We're just on our way to the bar—can I get you anything?' James offered.

'No, we're fine, don't let us hold you up,' Rob replied. His words were directed at James but he was looking at Ellie. His eyes were cold and hard, all traces of warmth gone from their green depths, and his stare made her feel uncomfortable. There was no invitation to join them, for which Ellie was grateful, but she was aware of the tension in the air and wondered whether James or Penny noticed it too.

James had. 'Well, that was awkward,' he said as they made their way to the bar.

'Mmm. Maybe they just wanted some alone time.' She almost mentioned their daughter but caught herself just in time. She didn't want to advertise the fact that she knew anything personal about Rob. Standing at the bar, she could feel someone's eyes boring into her back. She'd bet it was Rob and the thought increased her discomfort at the situation. 'Do you think anyone would miss us if we left?' she asked in what she hoped sounded like a casual tone. 'You're welcome to have a drink at my place.' She didn't care if he thought her forward, she didn't want to stay here under Rob's scrutiny any longer.

'Sure.'

They left the bar and walked across the road to the Hill Street house. James's Jeep was parked in front of her neighbour's place and he stopped beside it, unlocking the back. He flipped open the lid of an esky that was stashed in the boot and pulled two small bottles of beer from the ice.

'This wasn't quite what I had in mind when I asked you home for a drink,' Ellie said.

'Don't you drink beer?' he asked as he closed the ice box.

'I do but I have drinks inside.'

He smiled at her and Ellie delighted in the way his smile lit up his face. 'It was my buy, though, and this fridge was freshly stocked today,' he said as he flicked the tops off the bottles.

'Mmm.'

'What do you mean, "Mmm"?'

Ellie laughed. 'I'm just used to men trying a bit harder to impress me.'

'Hey, you invited me over and, remember, you're talking to a man who's living out of his car. But there's an additional benefit to that,' he said as he dived back into the esky. 'I can easily up the ante when required.' He emerged with a glass which he handed to Ellie. 'There you go, but I figured if you were prepared to go on a date with me, when you'd already been in my car, you're probably not into embellishments. There's not all that much about me that's impressive.'

'I wouldn't say that.' From where Ellie was standing there was plenty to be impressed with. At some point today he'd had changed out of the shirt and trousers he'd worn to work and was back in his faded jeans and black T-shirt. The same outfit he'd been wearing on the night she'd first seen him. The hot guy. She had no complaints.

The old, wooden, front gate squeaked on its rusty hinges as James pushed it open. He held it for Ellie. 'Do you want to sit outside for a bit?' he asked. Tucked against the side fence was a garden swing and he inclined his head towards it. 'It's such a beautiful night.'

It was too. The night was clear and still and the stars danced in the sky. To the north and west they competed with the glowing lights of the city but to the east, where they hung over the ocean, they were shiny and bright.

She kicked off her shoes and sat on the swing, her feet curled up beneath her.

James filled her glass and clinked his bottle against it. 'Here's to getting to know one another a little better.'

His smile was full of promise and it was enough to make Ellie tremble in anticipation of things to come. All in good time, she reminded herself. Even though the kiss they'd shared earlier in the day had been enough to make her change her mind about dating him, she still needed to try to take things slowly.

James joined her on the swing. He sat sideways and pushed off the ground, setting the swing moving gently. He pulled Ellie's legs out straight, settling her feet in his lap. He held his beer in one hand and rubbed the soles of her feet with his other.

It was heaven.

'What would you like to know?' she asked.

He took a sip of his beer before replying. 'What's your favourite colour?'

'That's what you want to know?' That wouldn't have been her first question.

He nodded.

'Blue,' she said. Or maybe chocolate brown now, she thought as she looked into the dark depths of James's eyes.

'Your favourite food?'

'Limes.'

'Limes are not a food.' He laughed. 'You're supposed to say smelly cheese or crayfish.'

'Well, I can't think when you're rubbing my feet like that,' she protested.

'Would you like me to stop?'

'No.'

He wiggled each of her toes in turn as he recited what he knew. 'I know you grew up in Goulburn, you were educated by Catholic nuns, you like blue, you think limes are a food.' He grinned at her. 'You work as a nurse and most of your male patients would love to be in the position I'm in right now. But I still need more.'

'How much more?'

'Like why you don't want to date a doctor.'

'I never said doctor, I said people from our department.'

'Either way, you've crossed me off your list.'

'Let's just say I've had a couple of bad experiences lately.'

'What happened?'

'Some false pretences and a lack of honesty.'

'Surely you can't attribute that to the fact they were from the orthopaedic ward?'

'No, it could have been coincidence but they were both doctors and I expected better, I guess.'

'So, no chance for me, then?'

'In your case I'm prepared to make an exception.'

James raised his eyebrows. 'Really? Why?'

'Because you certainly don't seem to be pretending you're someone you're not. After all you're living out of your car and you have an esky for a fridge,' she teased.

'Hey, that's not fair, I only live out of my car sometimes. I have to be at the hospital at seven tomorrow morning and it's a hassle driving all the way across the city from Cremorne.'

'I'm not criticising you. You're one step ahead of me, I don't even have a car.'

'So my semi-nomadic lifestyle isn't putting you off?'

She shook her head. 'Honestly, after you kissed me this afternoon I'm prepared to overlook just about anything. I have never been kissed like that before in my life and I want more.'

'Why didn't you say so earlier?' He took her glass from her hand and put it on the ground with his bottle of beer. His hands cupped her hips and he pulled her forward, wrapping her legs around his waist, joining them together.

His hands were warm and his body was firm between her thighs. Ellie imagined that this was what heaven would feel like. Warm and safe and perfect.

His lips were warm as he claimed her in a kiss.

His arms were around her, holding her, protecting her, keeping her safe.

The kiss was perfect.

She closed her eyes and surrendered to the sensation of being thoroughly kissed by someone who knew what they were doing. She parted her lips, her tongue tasted his, exploring his mouth. His hand was under her shirt, fingers splayed, warm across her back. She leant into him as he deepened the kiss.

It was heaven.

CHAPTER SIX

THE tell-tale squeak of the front gate interrupted the moment as someone else came home. Ellie froze and broke the kiss, her lips suddenly cold now they were no longer under James's caress.

'Wha—?'

'Shh,' she whispered, cutting off his question. She didn't want to draw anyone's attention. The front of the house was dark, casting no light on the garden swing. She watched as Tilly opened the front door and switched on the passage light. No one else was home yet.

'Who was that?' James asked as Tilly shut the door.

'Tilly. She lives here too.'

'Anyone else I need to know about?'

'Jess you met, we went to nursing school together. Tilly and Ruby, they're also nurses at the hospital, and sometimes Adam. It's his house.'

'Lucky Adam. Why is he only here some-times?'

'He's a surgeon. He works with Operation New Faces so he's away a lot.'

'Adam Carmichael? This is his house?'

'You know him?'

'I've heard of him but I've never met him.'

'He's just headed off again otherwise I could introduce you.'

'I think I'd rather not meet him under these circumstances.'

Ellie frowned. 'What circumstances?'

'Kissing his tenant in the front garden of his property,' James explained. 'It's not quite the first impression I'd want to make.'

'Oh, and why is that?'

'You know what the medical fraternity is like. There's a definite hierarchy separating us junior surgeons from our more experienced and es-teemed colleagues and it's important that I give the right impression.'

'And what would that be?'

'Being dedicated and responsible, and it's a bit

hard to do that if the first thing they see is me kissing the nurses.'

'I know about the pecking order,' she interrupted before he could say anything else he might regret. At least she hoped he might regret his words. 'Are you embarrassed to be seen with me?' If she'd learnt one thing from Rob's betrayal it was never to accept a clandestine relationship again. She wasn't someone to be ashamed of.

'That's not what I meant. I've been bugging you to go out with me so of course I'm happy to be seen with you. I just meant that I would prefer to meet any senior surgeons when I'm in work mode, not in the middle of my recreation.'

Ellie realised she was being unfair. She shouldn't judge James by Rob's standards. She owed him an apology. 'Sorry, I didn't mean to jump down your throat.'

'Don't sweat it, I'd rather we didn't have any misunderstandings and I'm more than happy to continue this…conversation…' he smiled at her and the corners of his dark eyes creased with mischief as he ducked his head and kissed her softly on the lips '…another time but I probably should get going before the rest of your house-mates come home.' He stood up and then took her hand, pulling her to her feet. 'Can I see you tomorrow? Are you going to the Stat Bar? The orthopaedic ward has organised drinks to welcome Penny Coleman to Australia.'

There was no way she was going to *that* gathering. She shook her head. 'I'm not going. I've volunteered to do a late shift.' That was at least partly true and she could hardly tell him the whole truth—*it would be extremely hypocritical on my part to welcome her to town when I had an affair with her husband.*

'Then I'll meet you at the hospital at the end of your shift and walk you home.' Now that he'd had a taste for her he knew he wouldn't be able to stay away. She was the type of girl who would get into his system. She seemed vulnerable. No, that wasn't the right word, fragile was perhaps more accurate. Not in a sense that she was delicate, just that she was the type of girl who needed someone to take care of her. She'd been to boarding school then nursing college and was now sharing a house with four others but he'd bet she wasn't the house mother. She would be the one that everyone looked out for.

He took a cool shower when he got to the hospital but then spent the night tossing and turning, thinking about Ellie. He knew he would probably have to take things slowly, but he needed some way of taking the edge off his desire, if he had to wait too long he'd go crazy.

The following evening he made sure he was back at the hospital before the change of shift as he didn't want to miss her.

'Did you go to the Stat Bar?' she asked him when he met her on the ward.

She smelt like sunshine; warm and happy, and that was how she made him feel too. How on earth could she smell so good at the end of a shift?

He nodded. 'Briefly,' he said as he took her hand, hoping she wouldn't resist. She didn't and he was surprised at how good it felt to leave the hospital hand in hand with her.

'Are you going back?'

'If I don't get a better offer I might,' he teased. 'What are your plans?'

'I'm going home for a shower and something to eat. How does that sound?' She raised one eyebrow and the corner of her mouth followed in a silent invitation.

'Too good to refuse,' he said, quickening his pace just a little as they walked down the hill.

His hand was warm and familiar as he led her away from the hospital. She barely knew him, how could it feel so natural?

The cool evening breeze carried his lime scent to her. He smelt so clean and pure after the chemical smell of the hospital. She breathed in deeply, letting his fragrance eradicate all the lingering traces of the orthopaedic ward.

She could feel the humming, their unique bubble enveloped her. She knew she should resist but, just as she'd feared, it was becoming harder and harder. The more time she spent in his company the harder it was to ignore the attraction. She was struggling to fight temptation. She was falling under his spell and she didn't think she could resist much longer.

Did it matter? she thought. Did she have to resist?

No, she just had to make sure she didn't fall in love.

He wasn't 'the one' for her. He'd already said he never planned on getting married. He definitely wasn't the one but that didn't mean she couldn't have some fun. She just couldn't take it seriously. He could be a distraction, some light-hearted relief. As long as she didn't make the mistake of falling in love, it could work.

By the time they neared the house she could barely concentrate on walking. All she could think about was James's touch. His grip was firm yet gentle, his hand was warm and she could already imagine how his hands would feel running over the rest of her body, running over her breasts, her stomach and her thighs.

They were two houses away and she felt her pace quickening. James's steps kept time with hers. They were both hurrying now, both eager to reach the house, and that's when she knew she was in trouble.

They barely made it inside.

As she pushed the front door closed James turned her around and pinned her against it.

He had one thigh between hers and his hands were at her hips, holding her to him. He bent his head and Ellie closed her eyes as she breathed in his tangy lime scent and waited for his lips to meet hers. Her stomach did a slow somersault of desire.

She felt his breath on her cheek. It was warm and soft and disappeared as his lips brushed over hers. She opened her mouth to taste him and their tongues met and entwined, joining them together. Her hands wound around his back and his muscles were firm and sleek beneath her fingers as she leaned into him. She needed to use his strength to hold her upright and just when she thought her legs were going to give way her stomach rumbled and the noise echoed in the long hallway, loud in the quiet house.

James broke the kiss. He was laughing. 'Why don't you have a shower while I cook us something to eat? What do you have in the kitchen?'

'You're going to cook?' He was thinking about food? That was the last thing on her mind.

'If I want to keep you awake most of the night

it sounds like I'd better feed you first or you won't make it,' he said with a smile.

That sounded better, much more in line with her own rampant thoughts.

'I have no idea what's in the fridge but you're welcome to see. The kitchen is through here,' she said as she ducked under his arm and led him to the bottom of the stairs and pointed towards the kitchen. 'You're welcome to use whatever is in the big fridge—the little one is Ruby's.'

'She has her own fridge?'

Ellie didn't have time for detailed explanations. Everyone else in the house was used to the dual fridge system, so she kept her reply brief. 'She's vegetarian,' she explained, as if it made perfect sense. She didn't elaborate any further, she was on a mission. She raced upstairs and stripped off her uniform, throwing it into the laundry hamper. She pinned her hair up to keep it dry as there wasn't time to wash it, and jumped into the shower.

Clean and refreshed, she rummaged through her underwear drawer. She had a bit of a thing for lingerie and only ever bought matching bras and knickers, as impractical as that often was. She found her favourite set and pulled it on. She sprayed her wrists and the backs of her knees with perfume and dabbed some on her throat before buttoning an old white shirt over her underwear. There wasn't much point in getting fully dressed, she hoped to be naked again very shortly.

She knew she shouldn't even be thinking about sleeping with James yet but she was finding him irresistible and perhaps the best way to get him out of her system was to take him to bed and then maybe the yearning would pass. She could do this. She could sleep with someone without falling in love and dreaming of babies. He wasn't planning on getting married so she could use him for sex with a clear conscience.

'Dinner smells good,' she said as she came downstairs. The smell of cooking had awakened her appetite for food and her hunger now almost outdid her sexual desire. Almost.

James was sliding omelettes onto plates and he looked up as she entered the kitchen. His eyes travelled from her face down along the buttons of her shirt to where the hem skimmed her bare legs and back again. He gave a low whistle. 'Wow, how quickly can you eat, do you think?'

'Let's start by putting the pan down,' Ellie said with a grin as she removed the frying pan from his hand. He was fixed to the spot and she recognised the fire in his eyes. She knew it was passion that made them burn like coal, turning them black.

James wolfed his omelette down in record time while Ellie sprinkled salt on her eggs and spread her toast with butter, teasing him as she ate her meal slowly and deliberately. She was desperate to feel his lips on hers, to feel his hands on her skin, but she knew it would be sweeter if she waited and she wanted him to want her just as badly.

But she hadn't counted on what he'd do while he waited for her to finish. What he'd do when he didn't have a knife and fork in his hands and food in front of him to keep him occupied.

He slid his chair closer to the corner of the table, closer to her. One hand disappeared under the table and she felt his fingers on her knee, just the lightest whisper of a touch but one that made her shiver with longing. His fingers brushed the inside of her thigh, inching higher and higher but, oh, so slowly. Ellie closed her eyes and breathed in, trying to control her senses, her meal forgotten.

The movement ceased. She opened her eyes, wanting to know why he'd stopped, wanting to tell him not to. His eyes met hers, even darker now, his irises and pupils all the same colour. He smiled, the corners of his mouth lifting very slightly before the smile broke open across his face. She knew then that he'd just been waiting for her to open her eyes, waiting to see his desire reflected in her. His hand moved again until it was merely inches from the top of her thigh. Ellie bit her lip and slid forward in her chair, pushing her hips towards his hand, urging him on.

James leant across the table, bending his head to hers, and his voice was soft in her ear. 'Are you ready for dessert?'

His lips nuzzled at her earlobe. Ellie nodded and tipped her head back, exposing her throat, and James pressed his lips to the soft spot under her jaw where her pulse throbbed to the beat of her desire. 'Sooner or later we're going to give in to this feeling,' he said as his fingers brushed across the fabric of her knickers. 'I think it might as well be sooner.'

Ellie couldn't argue. She couldn't even speak. She felt as though she was going to melt into the floor.

She pushed herself to her feet, taking her weight on the table as she wasn't certain her legs would hold her. James's hands moved to her waist and, for the second time in as many days, he supported her weight. She took his hand in hers and led him to the staircase. She gripped the banister as she concentrated on getting her feet to negotiate the steps. James followed behind her and she felt his hand on the inside of her thigh, connecting her to him as he trailed in her wake. She only just made it to the landing and into her bedroom.

James pushed the door shut and grabbed her hand, pulling her to him. His lips covered hers as his fingers popped the buttons on her shirt. She tugged his shirt out of his jeans and unzipped his pants, freeing him from the denim, before shrugging her shoulders out of her top. Her shirt fell to the floor and was joined by his shoes and jeans, and all the while their lips were locked as they feverishly touched and tasted.

He picked her up, as though she weighed nothing at all. She wrapped her legs around his waist and as he carried her to the bed she could feel his erection straining against his boxer shorts and she knew he wanted her as urgently as she wanted him.

She was wearing only her underwear; he still had too many clothes on. She reached out to him and slid her hands under his T-shirt, feeling the heat coming off his skin as she dragged his shirt up his back before pulling it over his head.

He bent towards her, kissing the hollow at the base of her neck where her collarbone ended. She tipped her head back and his lips moved down to the swell of her breast. She felt herself arch towards him, silently crying out for his touch. His hand reached behind her and with a flick of his fingers he undid the clasp on her bra and her breasts spilled free. He pushed her back, gently laying her down beneath him before he dipped his head and covered her nipple with his mouth. She closed her eyes as bolts of desire shot from her breasts to her groin. As James's tongue caressed her nipple Ellie could feel the moisture gathering between her legs as her body prepared to welcome him.

Her hands slipped under the waistband of his boxer shorts and she pushed them off his hips. His buttocks were round and hard under her palms.

James moved his attention to her other breast as she moved one hand between his legs and ran her hand along the length of his shaft. She heard him moan as her fingers rolled across his tip, using the moisture she found there to decrease the friction and smooth her movements.

She arched her hips towards him and he responded, removing her knickers and sliding his fingers inside her. She gasped as he circled her most sensitive spot with his thumb. He was hard and hot under her palm; she was warm and wet to his touch.

She was ready now. She didn't want to wait. She couldn't wait.

She opened her legs and guided him into her, welcoming the full length of him.

He pushed against her and she lifted her hips to meet his thrust. They moved together, matching their rhythms as if they'd been doing this for ever. She had her hands at his hips, controlling the pace, gradually increasing the momentum. James's breaths were short and she wasn't breathing at all. All her energy was focussed on making love to him. There was no room in her head for anything other than the sensation of his skin against hers, his skin inside hers.

James gathered her hands and held them above her head, stretching her out and exposing her breasts, and he bent his head to her nipple again as he continued his thrusts. The energy they created pierced through her, flowing from his mouth, through her breast and into her groin, where it gathered in a peak of pleasure building with intensity until she thought she would explode.

'Now, James, do it now,' she begged.

His pace increased a fraction more and as she felt him start to shudder she released her hold as well. Their timing was exquisite, controlled by the energy that bound them together, and they cried out in unison, climaxing simultaneously.

Never before had Ellie experienced the sensation of two people becoming one but there had been no way of separating the two of them, they had been unified by their lovemaking and it was an experience Ellie would treasure for ever. It had been everything she had expected and more. Their bodies had been made for each other.

Ellie woke at dawn as the first rays of sun hit her window. In their haste to tear off each other's clothes and get into bed last night she'd forgotten to close the curtains. James was lying beside her, still sleeping. He had his arm draped across her stomach but even without the contact she would have known he was there—she could feel the humming in the air and her room smelt of limes. It was almost as though even the particles in the air reacted to his presence. Nothing went unaffected, certainly not her.

She rolled onto her side to look at him. His face was relaxed and calm with just a hint of a smile tugging at the corner of his mouth. He stirred with her movement and opened his eyes.

'Good morning.' The smile that had been hovering at the edges of his lips burst across his face.

Ellie breathed out, relieved to see he was quite comfortable waking up in her bed and didn't appear to be looking for the nearest exit.

He rolled towards her and kissed her on the mouth. 'How did you sleep?'

'Short but sweet.'

'Sorry about that, I was enjoying our evening,' he said as his fingers found her breasts and started tracing circles around them, grazing her nipples.

'I'm not complaining,' she said.

She stretched her arms above her head, arching her back, and James groaned and ducked his head, taking her breast into his mouth and sucking on her nipple. His mouth was warm and moist and as his tongue flicked over her nipple Ellie felt it peak in response. She was ready for

James to make love to her again. It would be the perfect way to start the day.

She brought her hands down to his back and ran them along the ridge of his spine. She felt the small indentations at the base of his spine and kept her hands moving further until she could cup his buttocks. She slipped one hand to his groin. His erection pulsed under her palm. He was ready too. She pulled him over on top of her until his weight pressed her into the bed. He covered her body with his and she opened her legs, allowing him to join the two of them together again.

'You're going to make me late for work,' he said once they had satisfied their desires. Again.

'You could have refused,' Ellie replied.

He grinned at her. 'I didn't want to appear ungrateful.'

Ellie thumped him on the arm. 'Hey, watch it.'

'I couldn't resist, does that sound better?' he asked as he kissed her on the mouth, before sitting up and swinging his legs over the edge of the bed, preparing to go to work.

In a frame on Ellie's bedside table, just inches

from where he was sitting, was a family photograph.

He turned back to look at her as she lay on the bed. 'Are they your parents?'

She nodded.

'You've got your mother's eyes,' he said. 'Is it a recent photo?'

Ellie knew why he asked that. Despite the fact the photo had been taken twelve years ago her parents looked old enough to be the parents of a twenty-three-year-old. She shook her head. 'No. I was a late-in-life baby. They tried for ten years before they got pregnant with me. They were both thirty-nine when I was born and that was after several years of IVF treatment. They died in a car accident when I was eleven.' She picked up the photo in its frame. 'This was the last photo taken of them.'

'Oh, Ellie, I'm sorry.'

'It's okay, you didn't know.' She never normally volunteered the story of her parents' deaths, it was a part of her life she preferred not to revisit. Normally she would have only admitted that the photo wasn't recent and left it at that but around James things were anything but normal.

'What happened?'

This was her chance to say she didn't like to talk about it but instead she heard herself begin the story.

'We were coming back from the skifields—'

'We? You were with them?'

She nodded. 'We were coming down the mountain and we came around a corner and a grader was on the wrong side of the road. We ran into it and my parents were killed instantly.'

'And you? Were you hurt?' His eyes were roaming over her naked body, looking for scars and marks he might have missed while they'd been making love.

'Only minor injuries.'

'What about your siblings?'

'I'm an only child.'

It had been a long time since she'd revealed this much about herself in one conversation. Even Ruby, Jess and Tilly had only heard the story in bits and pieces. But she knew why she was confiding in James. It was partly because of the humming, that vibration that infused the air around them and made her feel as though they were encased in a private bubble, where time was suspended, and reality couldn't intrude. And it was partly because they'd had the most amazing sex of her life. If he could be that in tune with her physically she didn't think it could hurt to share some of her emotional self with him as well.

'That's why you don't ski any more,' he said. She nodded in response. 'So what happened to you then?' he asked.

'I went to live with Mum's parents.'

'And then to boarding school,' he filled in the gap. 'What about your grandparents, are they still alive?'

'My grandpa died a few years ago and my grandmother died recently. She was my last family member. I'm all that's left.'

'Just you? I had no idea.'

'Why should you? It's hardly a normal happy-families-type story. One day I'll have my own family, one day I'll belong to someone again, but in the meantime I have Jess, Ruby and

Tilly. They're my surrogate family.' And mean-while she could have some fun with James, she thought. 'What about you? What was your child-hood like?' She'd talked enough about her story.

'Not quite as calamitous as yours, maybe a bit closer to normal and relatively happy. I have an older sister, she's married with three kids. We were brought up by my mum.'

'What about your father?'

'Not in the picture.'

James had said 'relatively happy' but Ellie found the idea of an absent father unbearably sad. In her opinion, not knowing your father was worse than having a father who'd died. At least she had her memories.

He stood up. 'I'd better get moving. I'll grab a shower at the hospital.' He started picking his clothes up from where they were scattered over the floor. The conversation was obviously over. Ellie lay in bed admiring the curve of his but-tocks as he bent forward to pull his boxer shorts on. She could get used to this view. She just hoped she would get a chance to do it all again.

What if he wasn't planning on revisiting last night?

He was buttoning his jeans now and he turned to see her watching. He winked at her and her fears receded. He retrieved his shirt and pulled it over his head before he came back to the bed. He picked up a pen from beside the bed. 'Give me your number so I can call you later.' Ellie recited it and he wrote it on his hand before he kissed her goodbye.

She lay in bed, a smile playing around the corners of her mouth. It was okay. Everything was okay. He would call her, she knew he would. She'd see him again. He could be her transition man. She didn't have to fall for him.

'Doing the breakfast dishes already?' Tilly asked as she came into the kitchen to find Ellie with her hands in the washing-up water. 'Or are they last night's plates?' She looked from Ellie to Jess, who was sitting at the kitchen table. 'I know one of you got lucky, I saw someone sneaking out early this morning. Who has a confession to make?'

Ellie could feel herself blushing.

'Ah, Ms Nicholson, care to share? Who was he?' Tilly grinned and pulled out a chair, making herself comfortable beside Jess.

'James Leonardi,' Ellie admitted. She knew Tilly would get it out of her eventually.

'Who is he?'

'Do you remember the hot guy from the Stat Bar?' said Jess.

'I do!' Tilly's eyebrows shot up. 'The hot guy, wow. What's going on?'

Ellie shrugged. 'I'm not sure really, it's a bit soon to know, but I've never felt like this before.' Last night had been amazing but she wasn't ready to share the details yet.

Tilly raised an eyebrow and smiled. 'Really? You don't remember feeling like this with Rob and Nick and—?'

'I know what you're thinking.' Ellie knew that Tilly's list could go on and on and it was true, she did throw herself into her relationships and she tended to fall hard and fast. 'But it's different with James. We have a connection.' She knew that didn't come close to explaining how she felt around him but how could she describe the feeling, how could she describe that invisible hum of electricity that surrounded them both, the one she knew only they could feel? How could she describe the sensation of knowing when he walked into a room even when her back was turned? She was sure they wouldn't understand. She was convinced no one else had ever felt like this.

'I thought you were having a break from dating?'

'I'm not sure you could call this dating and I'm not going to fall in love and start dreaming about babies. He's already told me he's a confirmed bachelor with no plans to settle down. I've been forewarned. This is just a bit of fun.'

'Are you sure you know what you're doing?'

'Not at all,' Ellie confessed as she emptied the dirty water from the sink and dried her hands. 'But I can't seem to help it.'

'Promise me you'll be careful,' Tilly said as she stood up. 'I don't want you to get hurt again.'

Ellie grinned. 'Is that today's motto—if you can't be good, be careful?'

'Something like that,' Tilly replied.

'I will be, I promise,' Ellie said as Tilly hugged her.

Ellie wasn't sure how good or how careful she was over the next few weeks but she had a lot of fun. James was delightful company, attentive and funny, not to mention gorgeous and sexy. She was happy.

CHAPTER SEVEN

ELLIE was happy until Rob put a pin into her bubble of joy and popped it.

She was enjoying work, her initial reservations about dating another orthopaedic surgeon had worn off as she and James settled into a very easy relationship. James had no problem with people knowing they were an item and after dating Rob, when she'd had to be so careful to keep their relationship very private, this was a welcome change. She and James had lunch together as often as possible, he would meet her after work and walk her home whenever their schedules allowed it and even on the ward, while there were no huge displays of affection, there was always a touch of his hand or a wink or a smile to let her know he was thinking of her. Even with the hours he worked and the stress of his job Ellie found James to be very composed and relaxed at work and his attitude in turn kept her relaxed. She was even finding it easier to keep a calm head around Rob, or at least she thought so.

Ellie had paged Rob to sign Dylan Harris's discharge papers. After the debacle around George Poni's discharge she had decided to ask Rob first when his patients were ready for discharge rather than assume James could organise it. That way, it was Rob's decision and it helped to keep her head off the chopping block. She did her best to be efficient and succinct in order to keep Rob on side. She'd completed the paperwork and was standing beside him, handing him the relevant pages to sign, when James reappeared at the nurses' station after visiting a patient. He winked at her as he approached the desk and Ellie beamed at him.

'What time is your lunch break?' he asked. 'I'll try to meet you in the cafeteria.'

Ellie glanced at the clock on the wall. 'Twelve, I hope,' she replied.

'Okay, I'll catch you later,' James said as he headed for the lift, leaving her alone with Rob.

She watched James's back as he made his way along the corridor.

'You're still seeing Dr Leonardi, then?' Rob asked, interrupting her thoughts.

She was a little taken aback and wondered why it was any of his business but she had no reason to deny it. 'Yes.'

'You didn't waste any time.'

She knew she shouldn't get into a discussion about James with Rob at work or anywhere else but she thought his thinly veiled criticism was a bit out of line. 'What do you mean?' She couldn't stop herself from rising to the bait.

'Straight out of one bed into another.'

'How dare you?' Ellie fumed. 'I don't think you're entitled to comment, seeing as you had me in one bed and your *wife* in another at the same time!' They were alone at the nurses' station but Ellie was conscious of keeping her voice low regardless. She didn't want anyone to overhear this conversation.

'Not exactly. Penny wasn't in my bed, she wasn't even in the country.'

'She's still your wife and you were having an affair.'

'Information which I'm sure you would prefer to remain between us. As would I. You're not planning on creating waves, are you? That could make things awkward.'

'Awkward how exactly?' Ellie said through gritted teeth.

'You're a good nurse, I'm sure the hospital wouldn't like to lose your services.'

'You'd get me fired?'

'I don't think that would be necessary but if people got wind of your indiscretion you might find it embarrassing to continue working here.'

'*My* indiscretion!'

'I know I'm not the first doctor on staff who's welcomed you into his bed and I'm obviously not the last.' He shrugged. 'Who do you think is going to look like the victim?'

Ellie wanted to slap him. How dare he threaten her? She clenched her fist and stiffened her arm, forcing it to stay by her side. Slapping Rob wouldn't help matters—he'd probably charge her with assault. 'Don't worry, no one's going to hear anything from me,' she seethed, before turning on her heel and storming off. She was furious, she needed her morning tea break, she needed a chance to get outside into the fresh air to clear her head.

She was amazed, again, at how badly she'd misjudged Rob's personality. What bothered her, though, was what her misjudgement said about her. Was she really such a bad judge of character or had he kept the real Rob very well hidden?

She was still upset about his comments at lunchtime and on several occasions she almost mentioned something to James before she caught herself. She wasn't confident that Rob's threats were empty ones and she didn't want to chance her luck. It would be just her misfortune that he'd meant every word he'd spoken.

But the following day Ellie still couldn't help but replay the conversation in her mind and it bothered her just as much. She and James both had the day off and he was making her lunch at his house. She was hugely excited because she was finally getting to see where he lived but Rob's threats were overshadowing the occasion and making it difficult for her to fully enjoy the moment.

'You're very quiet. Are you okay?' he said as drove her from the farmers' market, where they'd shopped for ingredients for lunch, to his house.

She was tempted to tell him about Rob. She wished she could discuss it with him, wished she could ask his opinion. She knew if someone else knew about Rob's threats then it would be that much harder for him to get rid of her if he ever felt like it. But she was more afraid that Rob would carry through with his threat regardless so she kept silent.

'Yes, yes, I'm fine. Just imagining what your house looks like,' she lied. She forced herself to smile and tried to push thoughts of Rob to the back of her mind. She didn't want unpleasant thoughts to spoil her day any longer.

'Imagine no more, this is it,' James said as he pushed a button and a garage door began to open.

The house was not at all what she had expected. It was a narrow, modern, two-storey building. The garage door and front door were polished wood but the house itself was rendered brick.

James parked his Jeep and lifted a large cardboard box out of the boot. Piled into the box were a selection of mushrooms, a huge loaf of bread, cheeses, pâté, olive oil, fresh pasta and a lime and coconut pie he'd selected at the market. Ellie had been amazed at the amount of produce he'd bought but he'd just told her she'd understand why when she saw the state of his fridge and pantry.

She carried her purchase, a bunch of irises, and followed him out of the garage to the front door. James put the box down to open the door, letting Ellie enter the house first. The hallway was narrow and a few paces inside a staircase, with stainless-steel railings and steps in the same polished wood as the front door, led to the floor above.

'Head up the stairs,' he told her. 'The living areas are up there.'

Ellie followed his instructions and as she reached the top of the stairs the narrow confines of the house gave way to a magnificent open-plan living area with the most amazing harbour views. It was sensational.

'Wow.' The view led her to the front of the room where glass bifold doors opened onto a balcony. Still carrying the flowers, she went to stand by the doors. 'The view is incredible.'

James had put the box onto the kitchen counter and was standing beside her. 'I guess it is.'

'You guess! I can't believe you stay at the hospital instead of coming home to this. Don't you miss it?'

James shrugged. 'I leave home when it's dark and usually get back when it's dark too so I don't get to see the view that often.'

'Can we eat lunch out here?' Ellie looked around, searching for a table. There was a barbecue and a small outdoor setting on the balcony but although there was space inside for a dining table there wasn't one. There was a leather modular lounge, a flat-screen television, a bookcase and a few stools at the kitchen counter but that was it for furniture. It looked like they'd have to eat outside unless James planned on having them perch on the kitchen stools. Ellie knew the minimalistic look was the latest trend but she always thought houses looked a bit better with a bit of clutter. It gave them personality, made them looked loved.

Ellie then realised she was still carrying the flowers. 'Do you have a vase I can put these in?'

'You can check the kitchen cupboards while I pour us a glass of wine if you like.'

Ellie opened several cupboards, surprised to find most of them were only half-full. The cupboard above the fridge, which was where she would keep vases, was empty. The alcove for the fridge was huge and she had to stand on tiptoe to open the cupboard, although the fridge in place was only a small bar fridge. James opened the fridge as Ellie continued a fruitless search for a vase. He removed a bottle of wine and Ellie could see that, apart from wine and beer, there wasn't much else in there. If that was his only fridge, she could understand why he'd bought so much at the market.

She finally gave up looking for a vase when

she found a jug. She filled it with water and decided it would do.

The lack of possessions made her wonder if James hadn't lived here long. Maybe he was still unpacking. 'Have you just moved in?' she asked as she put the jug of irises onto the bench and took the glass of wine he handed her.

'No, I've lived here for a few years but I'm thinking of selling.'

She wondered why he hadn't bothered buying furniture but she supposed he had his reasons. 'How can you bear to move away from the views?'

'There are plenty of views around Sydney if you can afford them. This was convenient when I worked at the Royal North Shore but driving across the harbour is a hassle, even with the tunnel. I want to be closer to Eastern Beaches.'

Ellie pulled out a kitchen stool and swivelled it so she could see both the view and James, where he stood beginning preparations for their lunch. 'But where's all your furniture?' Her gaze travelled around the room again. Everything was in neutral shades, stone, latte and white, and even the modern sofa was in neutral, stone leather, plain and simple without any decorative cushions to give it some added colour. Even some aqua- or maybe lime-coloured cushions on the sofa would give the room a lift, she thought.

The tiled floor was clean but cold; there was one small, white rug in front of the sofa but no coffee table. Several of the walls were blank, their clean expanses broken only by empty hooks, hooks that must have remained after the paintings had been removed. There were a few photos scattered around and some childish artworks in primary colours covered one section of the wall but even these were arranged haphazardly. 'Have you "decluttered" to put in on the market?' she asked.

'My ex took half of everything.'

'Ex? When?' Ellie wondered how long James had been living in this sterile atmosphere. She couldn't imagine living like this for more than a couple of weeks. Had he been in a relationship very recently?

'A few months ago,' he said as he put a platter of cheese, pâté and biscuits in front of her.

'When I called off the wedding she decided she deserved some compensation and she took it in the form of the furniture.'

Ellie nearly choked on her wine. 'You were engaged?' Hadn't he told her he was never getting married? An ex-girlfriend she'd expected but an ex-fiancée was a bit of a surprise.

'Is she going to get half the house too?' Was that why he was selling?

'No. I was lucky.' He shrugged. 'She could have argued that after being engaged for two years she was entitled to more. I was happy to give her the furniture in exchange for my independence.'

Forget the furniture, Ellie thought. What was the point of a two-year engagement? Surely the idea of an engagement was to get married. 'Two years! Who has a two-year engagement?' she asked.

'Not many people,' he admitted.

'What happened?' Ellie hoped he wouldn't mind talking about it. After all, he'd brought up the topic.

'I'm not sure. We were both really busy at

work, she's a doctor too, and I guess I thought we had plenty of time. There was no hurry. But as our friends who got engaged after us started getting married before us she started to get into the whole wedding frenzy. And when she wanted to set a date I realised I just couldn't do it.'

'What do you mean, you couldn't do it?'

He shrugged. 'Our relationship had lost all the spark it'd ever had. And when we realised that, I realised I didn't want to fix it. I was concentrating on my career, expecting our relationship to take care of itself, and when that wasn't the case I realised I didn't really care enough to change. I didn't want to commit. I didn't want to make more of an effort. When I thought about it honestly I couldn't imagine spending the rest of my life with her. I realised I didn't love her and I knew that if we got married we'd end up divorced.'

'Why on earth did you get engaged in the first place, then?'

'I don't know.' He paused for a moment, as though trying to remember his reasons. 'She moved in and it seemed like the next step in our relationship.' He paused, as if trying to remember just what had gone wrong. 'I think all relationships go the same way. They start off as all consuming and you can't possibly expect that to last. That's why I'm not planning on getting married. I nearly made the mistake once and only a fool makes the same mistake twice. Marriage isn't for me.'

Ellie tried to put a positive spin on his revelation.

He was single, he was gorgeous and whether or not he thought he was marriage material was of no consequence to her. In fact, it was perfect. He was just what she needed to restore her confidence in herself and in men. He was honest and sexy and into her. He made her feel beautiful and, after Rob's deceptions had destroyed her confidence, James's attention was helping to restore it.

It didn't matter to her whether he intended to get married or not, he was only in her life temporarily. She was trying to live in the moment. She didn't need to waste time imagining a future with him. He'd made it perfectly clear where he stood on that issue, so all she needed to do was enjoy him. She knew the rules. She could handle this.

'How are things with you and James?' Jess asked as she and Ellie climbed into Adam's car. Adam was overseas again after a brief visit home and they were borrowing his car as it was the only one at their disposal and they needed to get to their wine-appreciation class. This was the fourth class in the programme but they'd missed the second because Jess had had a clash with her shifts and the third one as Ellie had gone out with James. 'I assume it's all going well seeing as I've hardly seen you for a few weeks.'

'It hasn't been that long, has it?' Ellie replied as Jess turned out of Hill Street and headed towards Bondi.

But Ellie knew Jess had a valid point. In the weeks since James had first kissed her, in the weeks since they'd first slept together, she knew she'd been swept up in the excitement of a new relationship. It was her way. It was all-consuming. When she was with James he was all she could think about and when she wasn't with him he was still all she was thinking about. It was only through sheer force of will and habit that she was able to stay focussed at work but when he was on the ward with her, when she was sur-rounded by their bubble, it was terribly difficult.

'Is he going to meet us at the Stat Bar later?'

Ellie shook her head. 'I don't think so. He's having dinner with his mother.'

Jess gave her a sidelong glance. 'Is that why you can make it to the class tonight?'

Between work and James she hadn't had a lot of time for her friends. She knew she'd been neglecting them but she wasn't strong enough to deny herself the pleasure that was James so whenever he was available she was with him.

'Yep, sorry.' Jess was right: if James had been free Ellie probably would have ditched the class in his favour.

'Don't apologise. I'm guessing the sex must be good: he's certainly keeping you occupied.'

Ellie laughed. 'The sex is fantastic but it's about more than that. I feel like we belong to-gether. Like I belong with him.'

'And you didn't feel like that with Rob?' Jess asked as she flicked the car headlights on.

'Not really. I never really knew where I was with Rob. I never knew when I would see him and it was all very secretive. I thought it was just his reserved English nature and I thought it was sweet that he wanted to keep me to himself but there was always part of Rob that he kept locked up and now I know why. Obviously there was a lot of stuff he was hiding but with James everything just feels open and honest.'

'So he doesn't have a wife and kids stashed somewhere?'

'Not that I could see,' Ellie replied. The ex-fiancée didn't count, there was no need to mention her. 'We talk about everything.' They spent almost as much time talking as they did making love and she felt they had no secrets.

'So he knows you want to get married and have babies?'

'Okay, so there are a few things he doesn't know about me but they're irrelevant.'

'Irrelevant! For as long as I've known you, your primary goal has been to get married and have a family. Don't you think you might be setting yourself up for more heartache if ultimately he doesn't want the same things as you?' Jess asked.

'We're just having fun. Those things don't matter.'

'Since when?'

'Since I'm trying something different. Remember, I've taken your advice. I'm choosing a man because he's a good man, not because he'd make a good father.' How could she explain there was no reason to tell him about her plans when he'd made it perfectly clear he never intended to get married? 'He's my experiment. I don't expect that the chemistry we have can last, it's too fierce. It burns like a supernova. So there's no need to tell him about my future plans. I expect he'll be long gone by then.'

Jess turned the car around a corner and veered wide to get past a van that was parked very close to the intersection. 'Mmm,' she said as she glanced at Ellie, 'just make sure you don't fall in love with him before the attraction extinguishes itself, then.'

Ellie was pretty sure she had things under control. Knowing James didn't plan on getting married had immediately changed her perception of their relationship. Her heart was safe, she thought. She wasn't going to fall in love.

Out of the corner of her eye she saw a flash of movement. Someone was running. Running straight towards them. 'Look out!' she yelled, but her warning was too late. Too late for them and too late for the jogger.

She heard a thud as the jogger collided with the front left corner of the car before bouncing off the vehicle. Ellie was thrown forward against her seat belt as Jess slammed on the brakes. She saw the man fly backwards and land on the kerb in a tangle of bloodied limbs. Long, lean limbs. Long, lean limbs, olive skin and curly dark hair.

'Oh, my God. James.'

CHAPTER EIGHT

Jess pulled the car to a stop at the kerb. Out of habit Ellie made the sign of the cross with one hand while she undid her seat belt and threw open the car door with the other. 'Call an ambulance,' she said to Jess as she jumped out of the car and slammed the door behind her.

Her heart was in her throat as she darted to the sidewalk. 'James?'

She knelt down beside him.

The crumpled figure lying on the edge of the road was a boy, not a man.

It wasn't James. A surge of relief flooded through her even as she acknowledged that this person was still injured and still needed her help. His right leg was twisted at an awkward angle and he had a dazed expression on his face. He was looking at her but Ellie was certain he wasn't really seeing her.

She put one hand on his bare arm, making contact, trying to get him to focus. 'My name is Ellie. I'm a nurse. I think you've broken your leg but I need to know if you're hurt anywhere else.'

There was still no reply but neither was there silence. Ellie could hear music and she realised then that the boy had headphones in his ears and one had fallen out. It was his music she could hear playing.

Was that why he wasn't responding? Couldn't he hear her? She reached over and removed the other earphone, letting it hang, just as Jess arrived.

'Are you all right? I'm so sorry, I didn't see you until you were right in front of us.' Jess crouched down beside Ellie as she spoke to the still silent youth.

'Did you call the ambulance?' Ellie asked her.

Jess nodded. 'They're on their way.'

'Do you think there's a blanket in the car? We need to keep him warm.' He was wearing a thin singlet and shorts, running clothes, and Ellie knew his body temperature would drop quickly with the combination of the cool evening air and the shock. Jess returned to the car to see what she could find.

Maybe shock was the reason he wasn't talking. She kept trying to elicit a response. 'Can you tell me your name?'

'Harry.'

Finally she was getting somewhere. 'Okay, Harry, other than your leg, can you tell me if anything else hurts? Can you move your fingers for me?'

Harry opened and closed his fists.

Maybe simple questions were the way to go. 'What about moving your elbows?'

He turned his head to look at her and Ellie had another flash of recognition. There was definitely something about him that reminded her of James. They had similar colouring and the same lean frames but it was more than that. Maybe the angle of his jaw or the way he held his head was familiar but she couldn't immediately pinpoint it. Harry had straightened his right elbow but as he attempted to repeat this movement on his left side he gasped with pain and Ellie's attention was brought back to the matter at hand.

'Where does that hurt?' she asked.

'My shoulder.'

'Okay, we'll leave your arm for now.' Ellie touched his left leg, 'Try to move your foot on this side for me. Can you move it around in a circle?' She knew he'd done some damage to his right leg, her guess was a fractured tibia, but she wanted to know if his left side had escaped unscathed. Harry managed to complete that movement without significant discomfort just as Jess returned with a beach towel.

'This was all I could find,' she said as she draped it around his shoulders.

'That'll do,' Ellie said.

She could hear sirens approaching and she hoped that waiting for ambulances wasn't going to become a regular occurrence for her. It was only a few weeks ago that she and James had waited for the ambulance in Kings Cross and Ellie could scarcely believe how much had happened since then.

The ambulance turned into the street closely

followed by a police car. As the paramedics emerged from their vehicle Ellie met them to hand over Harry's care and Jess approached the police to give them a statement. Ellie saw the police breathalysing Jess and she thought it was lucky they'd been on their way to the wine-appreciation class, not on their way home afterwards, although she knew the few sips they had while tasting wouldn't have caused problems. She knew they weren't going to make the class at all now, there would be no point by the time they'd finished up here.

The paramedics attended to Harry and took him off to hospital, where the police would get a statement from him later, but in the meantime they got a second statement from Ellie to confirm Jess' story.

'I saw him, but not in time to warn Jess. He just appeared from nowhere, well, from behind that van,' Ellie explained, pointing to the white van behind them. 'He ran straight out into the road, he didn't stop to look. He had headphones in his ears, and was listening to music.'

'How do you know that?'

'Because when I got out to help him I could hear the music coming through his headphones. It was pretty loud, I doubt he would have heard our car coming.'

The policeman jotted the details in his notebook before checking Jess's breathalyser results. He turned to her. 'Your blood-alcohol reading is 0.0. You're free to go but you'll both need to come into the station in a day or two to sign your statements when we've had a chance to type them up.'

Ellie and Jess did a quick inspection of Adam's car. There was a dent in the front passenger side panel but nothing that would stop them from driving home.

Jess pulled a face. 'Do you think he'll go spare?'

'No, it's just a car. He'd be more worried about the kid we hit,' Ellie replied.

'I wonder how much it'll cost to repair.'

'I wouldn't worry, his insurance should cover it. If we need to we can split the excess,' Ellie said as she opened the driver's door. 'Come on, I'll drive us home.'

* * *

James headed straight for the orthopaedic ward in the morning. He was worried about Ellie. When she'd phoned to tell him about the accident he'd offered to leave the dinner he was having with his mother to make sure she was okay, he knew his mum would understand, but Ellie had insisted that both she and Jess were fine and the boy they had hit would be okay too. But still he'd been worried. He knew it could be several hours before the reality of the episode sank in and he was worried about the girls going into shock.

Knowing Ellie and Jess had company in the form of Tilly and Ruby had eased his conscience slightly but he still wanted to see her this morning, just to make certain. It was Ellie's sense of fragility that bothered him. That feeling he had that she needed looking after. He thought he knew the reason behind it now—her family history would have contributed, he was certain—and even though she had her surrogate family, he wanted to be the one she turned to. He couldn't imagine what it would be like to be totally alone in the world and he wanted to be the one she could depend on.

He wondered when he'd made that decision. At work he was happy to have that responsibility, he'd been trained for it. He'd done years of study to equip him for those situations but he didn't want the same responsibility in his personal life. What if people depended on him and he let them down?

But it was different with Ellie. At least for the moment. He was prepared to be the one for her, for now. Short-term commitment was all he was thinking about. It was all he could offer.

He saw her the minute he stepped out of the lift. She appeared to be pacing the ward and the moment she sighted him she flew to his side.

'James!' She grabbed hold of his arm. 'Come with me.' She pulled him into the doorway of the doctors' lounge, out of the way of the main corridor and out of the way of the passing parade of people.

'What's the matter?'

'That boy we hit last night, he's been admitted to the ward.'

He knew the boy had sustained orthopaedic injuries and it was no surprise that he would be in this hospital, Eastern Beaches was the closest facility, but Ellie's brow was furrowed with concern and there was a small crease above the bridge of her nose. James wondered if the boy's injuries were more serious than they'd first thought. He wondered if that was going to cause a problem for Jess. 'Is there a problem?'

'I'm not sure. His name is Harry, Harry Leonardi. Do you know him?'

'Leonardi?' They had the same surname? James thought for a moment before shaking his head. Harry Leonardi wasn't a name he was familiar with. 'No, I don't think so.'

'Oh, I thought he might be related to you.'

'I've never heard of him. I'm sure there are plenty of Leonardis in Sydney.'

'But he looks just like you.'

'In what way?'

'He's got the same build as you, he's quite lean and his eyes are dark chocolate brown, like yours.'

'That could describe about a quarter of the males in Australia,' James said.

'I guess so,' she agreed.

'Was that all?' He should have bitten his tongue but it was too late, the words were out. He shouldn't have asked. He didn't want to know. But Ellie was telling him.

'It must be more than that 'cos he definitely reminds me of you. His smile is different but maybe the shape of his face...'

'Well, it doesn't really matter how similar we look, I've still never heard of him.'

'It's weird, though. He's almost the spitting image of how I imagine you would've looked at the same age.'

'What do you mean?'

'He could be a younger version of you.'

James could feel the blood drain from his face. 'How much younger?'

'He's fifteen.'

Fifteen years younger.

The hollow feeling in his gut was back. A feeling he'd first experienced eighteen years ago. As though someone had punched him hard enough to wind him and at the same time had ripped his heart out. He swallowed hard and forced himself to take a breath.

'Fifteen? What's he doing on our ward—shouldn't he be in Paediatrics?' He tried to concentrate. This 'Harry' wasn't an adult, he shouldn't be here.

'His growth plates are fused, and in Orthopaedics that means he's treated as an adult.'

James knew that was hospital policy but the shock had made him overlook the obvious explanation.

'Who is the admitting doctor?' he asked, mentally holding his breath while he waited for the answer, hoping it wasn't Rob Coleman. That could mean *he* could end up being responsible for this patient. Responsible for a fifteen-year-old boy with an identical surname.

'Bill Abbott,' Ellie answered.

Good. With any luck this Harry Leonardi would be a random stranger and nothing at all to do with him.

'Which room is he in?' he asked. There was no reason for him to cross paths with this patient or with any of his visitors but he'd make sure he kept well out of the way. Just in case.

'He's in Bed Twelve. Did you want to see him?' Ellie offered.

'No!' he replied as his pager buzzed on his hip. He'd heard enough about Harry Leonardi. He wanted nothing to do with him. 'I'd better answer this, I'm due in Theatre,' he said as he backed away quickly, leaving Ellie standing in the corridor with a slightly puzzled expression on her face. Perhaps she thought he was behaving strangely but he wasn't about to explain himself. 'I'll catch up with you later,' he said to her as he fled the ward in favour of Theatre. If theatre was as far away from Harry Leonardi as he could get then that's where he'd go.

Hours later Ellie was still puzzled about James's strange reaction to her ponderings about Harry Leonardi. She couldn't understand what the big deal was. She shrugged. So she thought James looked a bit like the kid. It wasn't a major drama yet James had reacted as if she'd handed him a live grenade. She wondered if he would mention the incident again tonight.

She looked in the mirror as she dusted eye shadow over her eyelids. She could see James's reflection in her bedroom mirror as she applied her make-up. He was lying on her bed, watching her get ready. He was dressed in an immaculate dark suit, a brooding contrast to the white linen of her bed and the colourful array of her discarded clothes that surrounded him. She'd tried on half a dozen outfits before finally choosing a simple black dress, which was now hanging on her bedroom door. She was wearing a bra and matching knickers. James was fully dressed. She leant forward to brush mascara onto her lashes and she could feel his eyes on her backside.

She looked at his reflection again and her heart skipped a beat. His eyes had darkened, they were almost jet black now. Their colour intensified in direct proportion to an increase in his level of desire. He didn't look like he was thinking about Harry Leonardi.

She wished she had time to take advantage of the hunger she could see in his expression but they were already going to be late for dinner. Normally that wouldn't bother her but it was a work dinner and she didn't want to turn up looking as though they'd just climbed out of bed. And she knew that was how she'd look. Her eyes would be bright, shining with satisfaction, her cheeks would be flushed and her lips would be swollen from James's kisses.

He was perfect. He was smart, gorgeous and kind. He was funny, gentle and honest. He was delicious. He was everything she'd ever dreamed of except for one thing. His only flaw was that he was a committed bachelor. But that was only a flaw in *her* eyes.

She knew he was only going to be a temporary man in her life yet she couldn't imagine her life without him any more. That was when she knew he was going to break her heart when he left her. And he would leave. If he didn't, she would. She would have to. She still wanted to get married. But first she'd have to get over him. But she didn't need to get over him just yet.

She watched as he shifted his gaze from her backside to her face, meeting her eyes in the mirror. She forced herself to break eye contact. James seemed to be able to read her mind and they really didn't have time to fool around before dinner. She picked up her lipstick and applied the colour to her lips, capping the stick as James checked his watch. He got up from the bed and crossed the room. He kissed the back of her neck and his hands were unusually cool on her shoulders. 'You'd better get dressed—we don't want to be late.'

Ellie let him zip her into her cocktail dress before she slipped her shoes on and took his hand to walk the short distance to the Coogee Surf Lifesaving Club for dinner to say farewell to the retiring CNC from the orthopaedic ward.

After main course had been served and eaten, Ellie stepped out onto the balcony that overlooked the Pacific Ocean. The balcony was deserted save for one solitary figure. As her eyes adjusted to the gloom Ellie realised it was Rob. James was fetching their dessert and bringing it to her but she had no idea how long he'd be and she had no desire to be alone with Rob. He was the last person she wanted to be trapped on a balcony with.

'Sorry, I didn't realise anyone else was out here,' she said and turned to leave.

'You're welcome to stay. Don't feel you need to leave on my account,' Rob said.

'It's okay, I'm going to go and get my dessert.' Ellie made an excuse and turned around and almost collided with Penny Coleman as she tried to make her escape. She had just enough time to see Penny register her face before she looked at her husband and judging by Penny's expression she didn't look happy with the situation. Ellie had thought being on the balcony alone with Rob was bad but it seemed the only thing worse was being out there with Rob and his wife. She tried to step around Penny but she blocked her path. Ellie stepped to the other side but Penny blocked her a second time. Ellie stopped.

'What are you doing?' she asked.

'I have something to say to you,' Penny replied. 'Stay away from my husband.'

Ellie frowned. Being on the balcony with Rob

had been perfectly innocent. 'What on earth are you talking about?'

'I'm warning you, I don't want you anywhere near him.'

'I—'

Penny cut her off. 'I didn't come halfway around the world to find my husband in bed with another woman, and if you think I'm going to ignore the fact that you were having an affair with him then you're sorely mistaken. I'm warning you—stay away from him.' Penny punctuated her words with a pointed finger, stabbing Ellie in the chest with her final few words.

Penny's grievance had nothing to do with tonight, Ellie realized, and she wondered how much Penny knew. She batted Penny's hand away. 'I think you should be having this conversation with Rob.'

'I have discussed this with Rob,' Penny said with a quick glare in her husband's direction. 'I've told him and now I'm telling you. Keep your hands off my husband.'

Ellie wasn't going to stand there and be bullied by Rob's wife. She bit back. 'I would never have got involved with him if I'd known he was someone's husband. Did he tell you he *forgot* to mention he was married?' Now it was her turn to glare at Rob. She couldn't believe he was standing there, mute. He'd obviously told Penny a version of events that suited him, though why he'd told her anything at all Ellie couldn't imagine. 'There was no sign that he was married, no wedding ring, and there was not one photo of you *or* your daughter in the apartment. I never heard him take a phone call from you and he never said a word until the end. Nothing. When he did remember to inform me I refused to see him again.' Over Penny's left shoulder she could see James walking towards the balcony doors. She had to get out of there. Quickly. 'I'm sorry that you two obviously have some issues and I'm very sorry that Rob has been unfaithful to you but I'm not the one to blame.'

She stepped around Penny and this time Penny let her go, turning to watch her leave. But before Ellie could escape from the balcony James appeared, carrying dessert. The air was thick with tension and James walked straight into the middle of it. This was worse than being trapped out here with Rob and Penny. *This* was now her worst nightmare.

James looked from Ellie's panic-stricken face to Penny's angry one. 'What's going on?'

'Nothing.' Ellie answered quickly, wanting to jump in before Penny had a chance to say anything. 'Can you just give us a minute?'

But Penny wasn't so easily deterred. She looked at James. 'They've been having an affair.'

'What?' James looked completely stunned. 'That's ridiculous. You can't accuse someone of such absurd behaviour. Ellie is my girlfriend.'

Oh, God, was he going to choose this moment to come to her rescue, to be her knight in shining armour? If the situation wasn't so disastrous she would have been thrilled at his announcement but under the circumstances she feared that the status quo was about to change. She couldn't bear to think that this was how James was going to find out about her affair. She'd thought it was probably inevitable but she didn't want it to happen like this, in a public showdown with the wronged wife.

'She might be your girlfriend now but who was she sleeping with before you? Ask her that! I don't want her anywhere near my husband.' Penny spat her reply at James before turning to Ellie. 'I'm going to get you transferred. You're going to be out on your tiny little backside.' And with those vindictive words ringing in Ellie's ears, Penny grabbed Rob's arm and dragged him away, leaving Ellie and James on the balcony.

Ellie was shaking. She couldn't bring herself to look at James. She didn't want to see the questions in his eyes.

'Is it true?' His voice was quiet but she could hear the hurt in his words. 'Did you have an affair?'

'Not exactly,' she said. She looked over the balcony at the ocean. The moon was reflecting on the water and she thought how beautiful it would all be if her day wasn't such a disaster.

'What does that mean?' James asked. 'Were you involved with him or weren't you? I would have thought it's a simple question with a yes or no answer.'

The truth was all she could give him. 'We did

have a relationship but I didn't know he was married. No one did.'

'And how is it that no one has been gossiping about you? You work in the same department, people must have known.'

'Rob was adamant that his private life stayed private. He said he didn't want to be fodder for gossip. No one knew we were dating. It was only when I found out he was married that I realised why he was so insistent on that.'

'How *did* you find out?'

'He told me a week or so before Penny arrived.'

'What happened then?'

'I called him all sorts of names and told him I wanted nothing more to do with him.'

James smiled then and it wasn't until that moment that Ellie realised how terrified she'd been that he wouldn't believe her. That he'd think she'd willingly have an affair. 'Were you ever going to tell me about it?'

'No.'

'Why not?'

'I was embarrassed, ashamed.'

'All those times that Rob was coming down hard on you at work, was that why?' James was leaning on the balcony beside her, their dessert abandoned on a table, forgotten. He put his hand on her arm and the warmth of his fingers cheered her. 'You should have told me then. I could have spoken to him.'

'I could handle it.'

'But you shouldn't have to. That's harassment. I could have stopped it.'

'He said if I told anyone about the relationship it would cost me my job.'

'He'd fire you? He doesn't have that power.'

'You heard what Penny said,' Ellie replied. 'I think he could make it happen or at the very least get me transferred to a different department. And I love my job, I wasn't going to risk that. The relationship was over, there was nothing to gain by telling you or anyone else about it. Nothing to gain but a lot to lose so I kept quiet.'

'Do you want me to speak to him now?'

'No!' Ellie just wanted to pretend that none of this had ever happened. 'That would just make matters worse. Please just let it go. He means nothing to me. The thing that bothered me most was not being able to talk to you when Rob had a go at me at work. Because of his threats I was too scared to say anything. I thought, if just one other person knew, it would be harder for him to get me sacked. And now you know. Now I can talk to you. That's all that matters.'

She turned towards him, seeking comfort in his familiar embrace. In her mind nothing would go wrong as long as she was with James. In her eyes he was as close to perfect as a man could be. She'd been so terrified of him finding out about Rob, knowing that part of her history, but he'd taken it all in his stride. He'd defended her. He'd believed in her. And that's when she knew her heart was in serious jeopardy.

She was falling for him. Despite all her resolutions, despite her bravado, she knew she was in danger of falling in love.

She'd have to be careful. She couldn't fall in love. She hadn't counted on that. And neither had James.

James was holding her against his chest. The top button of his shirt was undone. She stretched her hand up and undid the next button, and the next, and ran her fingers under the fabric and over the smooth, warm expanse of his chest. She kissed his skin. He tasted of limes.

'Shall we sneak off early?' she suggested. 'No one is going to miss us.'

His answering smile was the only encouragement she needed. She took his hand and escaped down the outside stairs. She would take him home. He would distract her and she'd forget all about Rob Coleman and his wife. She would share her bed with James and she'd try not to fall in love.

CHAPTER NINE

ELLIE usually slept soundly when James shared her bed but last night had been an exception. She'd been worried about his reaction when he learned of her dalliance with Rob and his calm acceptance of the situation should have reassured her yet she'd slept fitfully. The confrontation with Penny had frightened her and despite James's company she'd woken feeling exhausted.

She still had an hour to go on her shift but she could feel her eyelids drooping. She needed some caffeine if she was going to last until three. She was about to grab a coffee when Harry Leonardi's bell rang. She had to check on him first.

When she got to his bedside she was struck again by how similar he was to James. Their colouring was almost identical, the same black hair, chocolate eyes and dark, perfectly shaped eyebrows. His jaw wasn't quite as strong and he was lacking the shadow of a beard but that was possibly just the difference that age made.

'Sorry to bother you,' he said as she stood beside him, 'but I need to go to the toilet.' He gave her a slightly embarrassed grin and that was when Ellie could see a difference. A smile always transformed a face and Harry's smile was different from James's. Smiling, they looked less alike. Maybe she was being silly, she thought. Plenty of people had dark colouring.

She handed him a bottle and pulled the curtain around his bed to give him some privacy. 'I'll be back in a minute.'

Plenty of people had dark colouring but they weren't all called 'Leonardi', were they? And surely Leonardi wasn't a common name. She couldn't shake the feeling that there was a connection but James was adamant that he didn't know Harry.

She used the few minutes she'd allowed Harry to return to the nurses' station to check his notes. She flicked to his personal details, looking for his next of kin. Father's name, Antony Leonardi.

Mother, Lucinda Parsons. She wasn't sure what she'd expected to see but that told her nothing.

She felt, rather than saw, James arrive on the ward. The now familiar humming enveloped her just moments before his scent surrounded her. She quickly turned Harry's case notes over so he wouldn't see what she'd been reading. Not that it mattered. She was allowed to read them but knowing why she was looking through them gave her a guilty conscience. Her perusal had nothing to do with patient care and everything to do with her own curiosity.

James leant over her shoulder and kissed her cheek. 'Hey, gorgeous. How's your day been? Have you seen Rob?'

'It's been a good day actually. Rob was here earlier but everything was fine. I think that situation has been diffused.' It had been a huge relief when Rob had behaved as though nothing had happened. Ellie was hopeful that his threats had been empty ones. 'I'm going to grab a coffee in a minute—have you got time to join me?'

James shook his head. 'I've got to go back to Theatre. We're running behind on our list, but I wanted to check on Mrs Fisher and Julian Barnes and this gave me an excuse to check on you at the same time.'

'I'm fine, really,' she said as she pulled out the case notes he needed and handed them to him. 'Did you want me to come with you to check your patients? I just need to pop back to Harry Leonardi first.'

'No, no.' James took the case notes and stepped away from the nurses' station. 'I'm in a hurry, I'll be all right,' he said as he raced away.

Ellie shrugged. It wasn't like him to be hurried. The delays in theatre must have been worse than usual, she thought. She tidied up the nurses' station in preparation for handover before she went back to Harry to empty his bottle. As she approached his bed she could hear voices from behind the curtain. That was odd. She hadn't noticed anyone coming into this room.

'Harry, have you finished?' she asked, waiting for Harry's answer before she pulled back the curtain. The visitor was in profile to her and at first glance she thought it was James. But why would James have stopped here? Harry wasn't his patient.

The visitor turned to face her and she realised then he was a lot older than James but with similar build and colouring. This man must be Harry's father. He had the same lean figure and square jaw. Just as James's build was an older version of Harry's, this man's build was an older version of James's.

'Excuse me, is there an ice machine on this floor?' he asked.

Ellie pointed to her right. 'Down by the nurses' station,' she said. She should have offered to refill the jug for him but she was too surprised to think clearly. She frowned as Harry's father walked away. His gait was familiar.

Curiosity got the better of her and she grabbed the bottle from Harry and took it to the sluice room to empty so she could watch for Harry's father to return. She needed another look at him. She spied a linen trolley that had been left by the sluice room and pushed it along the corridor, using it for some cover as she continued to refold towels that didn't need refolding, waiting.

He was coming back now.

She tried to keep her gaze focussed on the stack of towels as she didn't want him to realise she was checking him over but he wasn't interested in her. He was looking straight past her, down the corridor. She saw him frown.

'James?' she heard him ask.

Ellie turned to her left, following his line of sight. James had come out of Mrs Fisher's room and was walking towards her, walking towards them both. He looked up at the sound of his name and Ellie saw him freeze in his tracks, a look of panic on his face. His eyes darted left and right as though he was looking for an escape. The colour drained from his face, leaving his olive skin pale. There was nowhere to go so he turned around and began walking back in the direction from which he'd come.

'James, wait.' The man called out again and started hurrying after James.

Ellie knew James hadn't noticed her. She was stuck to the spot, she couldn't make herself move and she couldn't look away. It was obvious that Harry's father knew James. There was a connection and she knew she was about to find out the answer she'd been seeking.

The man caught up to James and reached out and grabbed his arm. Not roughly but enough to make James pause. 'Please. Wait.'

Ellie glanced around. The corridor was still empty, save for the three of them. She saw James shake free of the man's hand. Should she call Security? She knew hospital procedure would probably dictate that she should but she still couldn't make herself move.

'Can you give me a minute?' she heard the man ask.

'What for?'

'I just want to talk to you.'

'I have nothing to say to you.'

'Please, listen.'

James shook his head. 'You're eighteen years too late. I'm not interested in hearing anything you have to say. Not any more.'

James walked away again and Ellie waited to see what would happen next. Harry's father took one step in James's direction before he changed his mind and stopped. He turned around and went back to Harry's room, still carrying the jug of ice chips.

Ellie jumped as the fire door at the end of the corridor slammed shut. James had found his escape.

Eighteen years too late. Was that what James had said? What did he mean? Ellie stopped pretending to fold towels and abandoned the trolley, and followed James into the stairwell.

He hadn't gone far. She found him leaning over the railing, staring down to the bottom of the flight of stairs.

'James?' She put her hand on his back. 'Are you okay? What's going on?'

He didn't lift his head. His gaze remained fixed, staring down into the abyss. 'Nothing.'

'That man, Harry's father, do you know him?'

James looked at her now and his expression was one of grief. 'I knew him a long time ago.'

Eighteen years.

It all fell into place for Ellie. The physique, the walk, the name. 'He's your father too.' *That's* why James and Harry were so similar. They were brothers.

But how could James not have known that? 'Did you know who Harry was?' He must have known, she thought. The only explanation could be that he hadn't wanted to tell her.

James shook his head. 'No. I suspected but—'

'Why didn't you tell me?'

'Because it doesn't concern you.'

His words pierced her heart.

'But he's your brother.'

'He's my father's son. That's not the same thing as being my brother. I don't know Harry and I've spoken to my father about twice in the last eighteen years.'

'*Twice* in eighteen years?'

'He left when I was young.'

Ellie remembered James telling her that his father wasn't in the picture. 'I got the impression you didn't know your father.'

'I don't.'

'But—'

James held up a hand, effectively stopping her question. 'I know you think everyone else has an ideal family, I get that, and I know your child-hood was far from perfect, but we didn't all grow up in a perfect world. My childhood certainly wasn't idyllic.'

'What happened?' Ellie wondered whether he would tell her or whether he'd tell her again that it didn't concern her. There was a long silence and just when she thought he wasn't going to break it he began to talk.

'Mum and Dad divorced when I was seven. Dad was moving to London with a lawyer he'd met at work, they were getting married. I found out when I was older that Mum had asked him to have marriage counselling, she'd wanted to try to save their marriage, but he wasn't prepared to do that. He walked out on her, on us, as quickly as he could and married Diane. But that marriage didn't last either. And then Dad met Lucinda. She was an Australian in London on a working visa. He divorced Diane to marry her and they came back here to live when I was about twelve. Dad hasn't been part of my life since I was seven.'

'But surely you saw him when he returned to Australia?'

'Once or twice,' James admitted.

Ellie frowned. 'Did he live interstate?' A shake of his head was the reply. 'Didn't he try to keep in touch with you?'

'For a while but I refused to spend weekends at his place. I refused to have anything to do with his new wife and eventually he stopped asking.'

'But why?' This made no sense to her. Why wouldn't James want to see his father? Why wouldn't his father insist they stayed close?

'I was angry.' James wasn't looking at her any more. He was staring into the distance, down the staircase, lost in the past. 'I thought he was moving back to Australia to be a father to my sister and me but it was because his new wife was pregnant and *she* wanted to come home. Dad wasn't coming back for us,' he explained. 'He'd replaced us. He didn't need us any more so I decided I didn't need him. I didn't want to have anything to do with him and his new family.'

'You knew about Harry?'

'I knew I had two half-brothers, Harry must be the younger one, but I've never met them.'

'Never?'

James shook his head.

'Aren't you curious about them at all?'

'No.' He looked at her then, just briefly. 'I don't want anything to do with my father and I don't want anything to do with his new family.' He took two steps down into the stairwell, obviously intending to have the final word. 'I need to get back to Theatre.'

And he was gone.

Ellie sank onto a concrete step as James disappeared down the stairs. The concrete was cold and hard but she barely noticed. She checked her watch. It felt as though hours had passed but it was actually only minutes. Her shift would be over soon and she needed to get back to the ward but she couldn't make herself move. She was stunned. She couldn't reconcile the conversation she'd just had with the person she thought she knew. Where had the considerate, thoughtful, generous James gone? The one who chose lime and coconut pie because he knew it was her favourite flavour, the one who massaged her aching feet at night, the one who brought chocolates to Hill Street for all the girls or spent the extra few pre-op minutes to calm an anxious patient. What had happened to him?

His reaction didn't gel with the man she thought she knew and if he thought he could avoid this topic by escaping to Theatre he was wrong. He couldn't pretend his family didn't exist. She couldn't let him. In her opinion there was nothing more important than family.

Ellie wandered aimlessly around the house. She couldn't relax, wound tight following the events of the afternoon. She grabbed a hat and left the house. Turning right, she headed for the beach. A walk would probably do her good, and the fresh air might clear her mind. She walked for over an hour, accompanied by her thoughts, but they didn't become any clearer. She was on the home stretch when she heard someone calling her name. James was coming towards her.

'I'm glad I found you.' He didn't give her a chance to say anything before he pulled her into his arms, hugging her tight. 'I'm sorry,' he said. His voice was muffled, his mouth was pressed against the top of her head, but she heard his words clearly enough. 'I handled things badly this afternoon.'

Ellie felt herself relax. The stress of the afternoon melted away under his touch, evaporating into the atmosphere, carried away on a breath of lime. He was back, the James she knew. Everything would be all right. She wrapped her arms around him as she let her head rest against his chest. His heart beat was loud in her ear. 'It's okay. I know it must have been a shock to see your father today. Eighteen years is a long time.'

'A shock is a bit of an understatement,' he said as he stepped back, taking her hand in his and leading her to a wooden bench that overlooked the ocean. He pulled her onto his lap.

'How are you feeling now?' He was holding onto her as if his life depended on it. He had obviously been quite thrown by the events of the day.

'I'm not sure. It's surreal really. I had an image in my head of how it would be if I ever ran into my father. What I would do. What I would say. But today was nothing like I'd imagined. Instead of behaving like a mature, thirty-year-old all I could think of, all I could feel, was the anger and hurt that I'd felt all those years ago.'

'Do you think you might want to see your father? Or Harry?'

James shook his head. 'No, that's not what I came to tell you. I have no intention of having a relationship of any sort with my father or his family.'

'You're going to ignore your own brothers, your own flesh and blood? How can you do that?' Ellie had been certain he would at least want to see Harry.

'My father left me. He walked out. As far as I'm concerned, he made his choice.'

Ellie was amazed. 'I would do anything to have someone to call mine, a parent, a sibling, a grandparent, a cousin even. Jess, Ruby and Tilly are the closest thing I've got to a family and they're fabulous and I'm very lucky but it's not the same. I can't believe you don't want to know them.'

'I have a family. I have my mother and my sister.'

'You also have two brothers. You have a sibling, right here, under your nose. Are you going to pretend he doesn't exist?'

'He's a half-brother. He's my sibling in name only.'

'I would always choose family,' she said.

'But I have two families to choose between. As did my father. He chose his new family and I'm choosing my old one.'

'But you're upset because your father *did* make a choice. Can't you see that by refusing to meet Harry you're repeating the pattern?' She tried to get him to see her point of view. Tried to get him to see that his reasoning didn't make sense.

'Just drop it, Ellie, this is not a decision you get to make. This has nothing to do with you. I don't know Harry and he doesn't know me.'

'Would you meet Harry if I asked you to?'

'I'm sorry, Ellie, I can't do it. Not for you, not for anyone. Surely you can understand. Can you imagine a father who would walk away from his family, leaving them without looking back? Off to start a brand-new life. Not once, but twice. What sort of a man would do that? That's not someone I want in my life.'

'But that doesn't stop you from getting to know Harry.'

'No, but Harry's a reminder that my father didn't want us. I don't need my father. I don't need any of them. Can you respect that it's my decision?'

Ellie was watching him as he spoke. She could see the stubborn set of his jaw, the muscle bulging below his ear as he clenched his teeth. He meant every word. His mind was made up and he wasn't going to be swayed.

Had she misjudged his character too? She couldn't believe she was such a poor judge of human nature. Sure, she'd been fooled by Rob but she thought that had taught her a lesson. But now James was showing her a side of him that she hadn't expected. Or was he? Had there been glimpses of this independent streak and she just hadn't been paying attention? Had she not been listening?

He'd said all along he was a confirmed bachelor and he had one broken engagement to prove it. She wondered how much of it was due to his father's track record—three marriages was a lot by anyone's standards. But had she ignored all his words in the vain hope that he'd change his mind? She knew she had. She knew she'd been hoping they'd have a chance of a future. But if he wasn't going to open his heart to his brothers, how could she hope he'd open his heart to her.

He'd always been honest with her. Perhaps he meant it when he said he didn't need a family.

But she did.

Her desire for family overshadowed everything.

She couldn't believe he could pretend his family didn't exist. She couldn't love a man like that.

Love? Where had that idea come from?

Did she love him?

She was quiet for a moment. Thinking. Feeling. That empty spot in her heart, that spot waiting to be filled, wasn't empty any more. James had filled it. She loved him.

But her idea of a family was more important to her than anything.

Was it more important to her than James? She

knew she couldn't have both but could she give him up? She didn't know.

Perhaps if he'd been willing to compromise, willing to meet Harry even, there would have been some hope. Hope that maybe one day he'd give up his bachelor life and choose a family of his own. But looking at him now he seemed so certain, so determined, and she couldn't afford to wait and see. It would only end in a broken heart. She needed to protect herself.

'You're right, it's your decision. I have to respect that but I don't agree. Family is more important to me than anything else.'

'Can we agree to disagree?'

She shook her head. 'I think I understand why you feel this way but I can't reconcile that with the man I thought I knew and it's at odds with everything I believe. I need some time to think.'

'What are you saying?'

'I don't think this relationship is going to work. I have to respect your decision but I can't abide by it. I can't see you any more, James.' Maybe she was being unreasonable but she couldn't open her heart to him any further. She couldn't take the chance. Only a fool would willingly give away her heart, knowing it would be crushed.

CHAPTER TEN

ELLIE was lying on her back on the garden swing. It was a beautiful day, not that she'd noticed. She had a hat covering her face, hiding her from the world like an ostrich with its head buried in the sand. She had one leg hanging over the side of the swing and every now and then she'd push off the ground with her toes, giving the swing a little momentum. She found the gentle rocking motion soothing.

She was supposed to be at work but she'd begged one of the other nurses to swap a shift with her. She'd had yesterday off but she needed another day. She couldn't face going back to the hospital.

Work had been horrendous and she'd spent most of her past two shifts fighting back tears. Working with James had been torturous and she'd struggled to get through the day. She had hoped he'd come after her. Had hoped he'd find her and tell her he loved her. Had hoped he'd tell her she was right and that he would get to know Harry. But, of course, he hadn't done any of those things.

Her heart couldn't cope with another day on the ward with him. Another day knowing he was no longer hers. She should have stuck to her plan of not dating orthopods. She should never have got involved.

She'd needed a 'mental health day'. A day to lie in the garden and wallow in her misfortune. Her heart ached. She'd never understood that expression before but she did now. She could actually feel her heart in her chest and it ached, just like a torn and bruised muscle, and made it difficult to breathe. She wasn't actually sick, there wasn't anything wrong with her that a doctor could fix. Not a regular doctor anyway. Her illness could only be cured by Dr Leonardi and she didn't think he was going to be around any time soon.

She heard the telltale squeak of the front gate as someone entered the garden. Fixing the gate was still on Tilly's to-do list. Tilly had visions of herself as a handywoman and she had a list a mile long of all the things she was going to fix in her spare time. The trouble was she hardly ever had the time even though she had the inclination.

Ellie lifted the brim of her hat and turned her head to see who the intruder was. Disappointment surged through her when she saw Ruby and Tilly coming through the gate. Despite everything, part of her had hoped it would be James.

The movement of the swing caught the girls' attention and they changed course and headed across the garden. Ellie sat up, making room for them to sit beside her.

'Hi,' she said, as she sniffed and rubbed her nose.

Ruby was peering at her, trying to see behind her sunglasses. 'Are you all right?'

'Not really,' Ellie admitted.

'What's happened?'

'Remember when Jess and I had the car accident and we hit that boy, the one who was jogging?' She paused, waiting for the girls to nod. 'He's James's brother.'

'Really? Why haven't you told us?' Ruby asked.

'Because I didn't know.'

'James didn't tell you?' Tilly responded, obviously thinking that was what had upset Ellie.

'He didn't know either,' she admitted. 'Well,' she clarified, 'he wasn't sure.'

'What do you mean, "he wasn't sure"? That doesn't make any sense.'

'His parents are divorced and his father remarried and had a second family. James knew he had two half-brothers but he didn't know one was Harry,' Ellie explained.

'I don't understand why this has upset you,' Ruby said.

'Because James doesn't want to know about Harry, he doesn't want anything to do with him.'

'But why are you upset about that? James must have his reasons. Surely he can do what he likes,' Tilly commented.

'James doesn't want to have anything to do with his own family!' Didn't *anyone* get why this was such a big deal? 'How could I have fallen in love with someone who has no need for family?'

'You're in love with him?' Ruby and Tilly spoke in unison.

'I thought he was supposed to be your transition person,' Ruby continued, 'your experiment?'

'He was but it hasn't turned out quite how I expected. He's the one I've been searching for. He's the one who makes me feel complete.'

'Well, that's a pretty good reason to try to work out your differences. Are you going to try to figure this out or are you going to walk away over a disagreement over a half-brother who means nothing to you or James?' The no-nonsense, practical Tilly was in full flight.

Ellie looked at Tilly. 'I told him that having a family was the most important thing in the world and if he wouldn't make an effort to get to know Harry then I didn't want to be with him.'

'So what? Apologise. Tell him you made a mistake. Tell him you love him.'

Ellie shook her head. 'I *do* love him and I could say the right words but it doesn't change the fact that I think he should meet his brothers and unless he's going to at least consider the idea of opening himself up, he's not the man for me.'

'You realise you could be in a no-win situation, taking that stand.'

'He knows how important family is to me. If family doesn't matter to him, I can't ignore that.' Ellie wasn't letting go of the hope, of the relatively slim chance, that James would eventually see her point of view, and agree with her.

'Well, in that case I don't see much point in lying around here, moping,' said Ruby. 'I think this calls for a session at the Stat Bar.'

'I'm really not in the mood,' Ellie objected.

'Rubbish, you need a distraction. We'll all get changed and head over there now.'

Ellie knew there was no point arguing and lying on the swing hadn't solved her problems, maybe Ruby was right. She did as she'd been instructed and changed out of her shorts into a dress and slipped her feet into a pair of wedges. She brushed her hair and slid an Alice band into it to disguise her hat hair—it was hard to look glamorous after a day spent lying in a garden swing.

A dash of make-up and a couple of quick vodka, lime and sodas at the bar and she began to feel a little more sociable. There wasn't really much point in hiding. Sooner or later she was going to have to face facts—James and she had a difference of opinion and it was big enough to tear them apart. He was only supposed to be her transition man, she'd get over him. Eventually.

She was sitting at a small table with Ruby when the air around her began to vibrate. She knew without looking that James had walked into the bar.

'He's here, isn't he?' she whispered.

She saw Ruby glance over her left shoulder and then nod her head.

Ellie took a deep breath. She could do this. She could be in the same bar as him. As long as she didn't have to see him it would be fine.

But he didn't stay out of sight. He walked past them on his way to the bar and his fresh, lime scent washed over her. She closed her eyes as his familiar smell pervaded her senses. When she opened them he was in her direct line of sight. He was standing at the bar and she was looking right at him. At the lean line of his spine, the firm bulge of a biceps and the curve of his bum in his jeans. He was wearing blue jeans tonight, not black, and a red polo shirt. The colour suited him, a nice contrast to his olive skin and dark hair. She ran her eyes over him, committing every inch of him to her memory.

He ordered his drink and then turned in her direction. He looked straight at her. She didn't think it was an accidental glance. He must have known she was there, he must have seen her on the way in. Their gazes locked. Ellie couldn't turn away. Even now that strange connection was still working and it was too powerful for her to overcome. It held her transfixed. James gave her the slightest nod but he didn't approach her. He picked up his beer and headed for the opposite side of the bar and her heart ripped a little more as he walked away.

So that was how it was going to be.

'Go and talk to him,' Ruby said, giving her a nudge.

Ellie shook her head. 'He needs to make the first move.'

'Why?'

Because I have my pride. 'Because I'm not going to let him brush me off again and tell me his family is none of my business. And if I go to him, that's what will happen. I'm moving on.'

'O-kay,' Ruby said with a tiny shake of her head and a mini eyebrow rise.

But despite her claims Ellie couldn't ignore him completely. His red shirt was like a beacon, continually drawing her gaze, and she couldn't stop herself from glancing in his direction no matter how hard she tried. The constant pull of attraction was a strong as it had ever been and she couldn't resist it.

'Oh, for goodness' sake, if you're going to sit here and try to pretend he doesn't exist we might as well move the party to our house. At least then you won't be able to keep sneaking glances at him.'

Ellie opened her mouth to protest. She didn't want to leave. She wanted to stay near him but as those thoughts entered her mind she realised how ridiculous she was being. Ruby was right. What was the point of sitting here looking at him if she wasn't going to speak to him? She closed her mouth and stood up.

Ruby, Jess and Tilly gathered up a bunch of friends from the bar and invited them all back to Hill Street. Impromptu parties were one of Ruby's favourite things and people had learnt to accept her invitations because it was always fun.

But Ellie dragged her feet. She didn't want to leave the bar, not while James was there. Being in the same place as him was better than nothing. Despite their differences she hadn't reconciled herself with the fact that it was over. She knew it was probably only a matter of time before their relationship would have run its course anyway. On several occasions she'd thought their attraction, their chemistry, was too powerful to sustain. Sooner or later it would exhaust itself, and them, but she wasn't ready for the end just yet.

She escaped to the kitchen on the pretext of mixing a jug of drinks. She didn't need any more to drink but it gave her an excuse to get away from everybody else. It gave her an opportunity for solitude and a chance to think about James in peace and quiet.

She crushed some ice and measured the vodka into the jug before adding some lime cordial and soda water. She grabbed a lime from the fruit bowl, selected a sharp knife and began slicing the lime to add to the jug. The kitchen filled with the scent of limes, immediately reminding her of James. For a small fruit it was very fragrant.

'Hello, Ellie.'

The sound of his voice made her jump. She looked towards him, needing to make sure she wasn't imagining things, and as her attention was distracted the knife slipped off the side of the lime, slicing into her finger. 'Damn it.'

That was why the lime fragrance was so strong. He was here, in her kitchen, leaning casually on the doorframe as if nothing had changed.

She dropped the knife and lifted her hand to check the damage. The cut was shallow but bleeding freely.

He crossed the room, moving quickly to her side when he saw the blood. He took her hand in his and led her to the sink. He turned on the tap and held her hand under the running water, rinsing the blood away so he could see the cut.

'I didn't mean to startle you.'

She didn't answer. She was staring at his hand as it held hers. She watched as the water ran over her finger, turning pink as it ran off into the sink. James's fingers were resting over the pulse at the base of her thumb. She could feel the pulse beating under his touch, as he held her wrist and turned the tap off.

'Does it hurt?' he asked.

She shook her head. She couldn't actually feel her finger. All she was aware of was his touch. The skin around her wrist was on fire and she could feel every beat of her heart as it pushed her blood through her body and out of her finger. Suddenly the image of all her blood running down the drain made her feel dizzy. Her knees wobble. Almost instantly she felt James's arm hug her around her waist as he lifted her off her feet and seated her at the table.

'Put your head down,' he said as he pushed her head forward, tucking it into her lap, holding it there with one hand while he held her left arm in the air with his other hand.

Ellie took some deep breaths, forcing the air into her lungs, and gradually she felt her head clear. Her senses were returning. She could hear and smell and feel but she still couldn't talk.

She felt James change hands and then felt him wrap a cloth around her finger. She looked up and her eyes met bare skin. He was using his shirt to stem the bleeding. He must have taken it off when he changed hands. She would see the ridge of his abdominals, perfectly formed under his smooth, tanned skin and she felt herself hyperventilate again.

'The cut's not too deep,' he said, 'I should be able to hold it together with sticky plasters. Where do you keep them?'

Ellie pointed to a cupboard above the stove.

'Keep some pressure on here while I get them down.'

His shirt smelt of limes. Ellie bent her head, immersing her face in his shirt and breathed in his scent, using the perfume to regain her focus. She lifted her head in time to see him stretching to retrieve the small first-aid box from the overhead cupboard. Her eyes were drawn to the curve of his back and the ripple of muscles around his shoulder blades. His beauty was breathtaking. She'd almost forgotten how graceful his movements were.

He came back to her, holding the box in his hands, and with every step closer her heart rate increased its pace.

He searched through the box, selecting a few sticky plasters of varying sizes before he unwound his t-shirt from her finger. The bleeding had stopped and he quickly taped the edges of the cut together before cleaning up the bloody knife and chopping board and throwing out the remnants of the lime.

Finally Ellie recovered the power of speech. 'What are you doing here?'

That was a good question. He hadn't really thought through what he was doing when he'd followed her home. He couldn't think of much at all once he'd seen her at the Stat Bar. Her presence had consumed his thoughts and he hadn't been able to keep his eyes off her. He had been conscious of her watching him too. Their eyes had kept meeting but neither one of them had been prepared to cross the room.

He'd thought he could distance himself from her, from her idea that all families were happy families, from her belief that he should get to know his brother. His half-brother. From her belief that he would *want* to know him.

But distance wasn't working. He missed her. The light had gone with her and his world was not as bright or as warm or as happy without her in it. He knew he should just let her go. He didn't need any complications. He didn't want to be in a serious relationship, one where they had discussions about their beliefs and desires and principles. He didn't want to get too involved with someone who'd made no secret of the fact she wanted a family of her own 'one day'. But he wasn't ready to give her up, not just yet. And that meant trying to find a compromise.

None of this was her fault. The situation between him and his father was not her doing and he shouldn't be blaming her for her perception of the circumstances. But that didn't mean he agreed with her. Not completely anyway. He didn't want anything to do with his father and he wasn't going to be persuaded otherwise. But he needed to make her understand. If he wanted her back in his life they needed to sort this out. He wasn't going to let his father ruin another relationship. His father had done enough damage to his own family and he wasn't going to let his father's actions interfere with any other part of his life.

He needed to talk to her but the Stat Bar was not the place for this conversation. He'd seen her leaving so he'd followed a few minutes behind, thinking maybe he'd have more luck getting a private conversation at her house.

He hadn't realised a crowd was going home with her and by the time he'd reached her house the garden and the lounge were filled with people. He'd used the crowd to his advantage, walking straight through the front door, unnoticed by everyone as he'd searched for Ellie. A brief glance around the garden and into the lounge and he'd known she wasn't there, he couldn't feel her.

He'd continued on to the kitchen and he'd felt her presence getting stronger as he'd got nearer.

She was watching him, waiting for a reply. What had she asked? *Why was he there?*

'I needed to see you,' he replied. He pulled out a kitchen chair and sat at the table. 'I want a chance to explain.'

'Explain what?'

'That family *is* important to me. I need you to understand something before you judge me.'

'I wasn't judging you.'

'Yes, you were. You were expecting me to embrace a family that I have no connection with. I understand your reasoning, but family to me is more than just blood relations. Family is the people who love you and support you through the highs and lows of your life. They are the ones you want to share things with and the ones you turn to when you need encouragement. My family is important to me but when I say family I mean my mother and my sister. They are what matters.'

'And what about Harry?'

'Harry is not my family. Harry is a stranger.'

'But he doesn't have to be.'

'We have nothing in common—'

'Other than your father.'

'Who I haven't seen in almost eighteen years. I don't need him and I'm sure he doesn't need me.' He ran his hands through his hair and took a deep breath. He needed to get this right. Ellie needed to understand his point of view. 'Not wanting to meet Harry doesn't make me a bad person. I have a family, my mum and my sister.'

She was shaking her head. 'I know your father's behaviour hurt you deeply but your father's behaviour isn't Harry's responsibility or burden any more than it is yours. You have a brother, two brothers, who you refuse to acknowledge, and I'd give anything to have just a little of what you're prepared to throw away. That's what I don't understand.'

'I can appreciate how hard it must have been for you to lose your parents, especially as an only child, but having a big family is not necessarily better than having a small one.'

'I would be grateful to have one at all.'

'That's my point. I'm happy with the family I

have. I don't need more than that. My family is not my father or his new wife or some half-siblings I've never met. I have a family and I want you to meet them. Would you come with me to my sister's house tomorrow? It's my nephew's birthday and we've been invited for afternoon tea.'

She was frowning. 'We? I've been invited? You want me to come with you?'

He nodded. 'I want you to meet my family, to see that I'm not a horrible, cold-hearted person. I want to show you that I do believe in family. I have a family that I love very much, a family who have loved and supported me my *entire* life. Please give me a chance to redeem myself.' He reached his hand across the table, imploring her to give him another chance. 'I've missed you, Ellie, please do this for me. For us.'

'You've missed me?' He was going to forgive her for their differences? Despite everything he still wanted her?

She remembered Tilly's words. *Are you going to try to figure this out or are you going to walk away over a disagreement over a half-brother who means nothing to you or James?*

Could she apologise? Could she say she'd made a mistake? Could she tell him she loved him?

She knew she could apologise. She could back down, relax her position on Harry, and perhaps, given time, he would see her point of view. She could hope for that and in the meantime it would give James back to her. But she couldn't admit she loved him. That wasn't going to happen.

'Come and meet my family and you'll see why I don't need more than them. Sometimes just one person is enough.'

He was leaning towards her and she could feel the heat radiating from him. She reached out with her right hand, wanting to touch him, needing to feel him. His skin was warm under her fingers. She could feel his heart beating and its rhythm travelled through her fingers, infusing her body with his pulse.

This was ridiculous. She could feel herself falling under his spell. She was letting him charm her with words. Letting his familiar scent persuade her to listen to him.

Maybe she should meet his family. If he was keen for her to see that side of him, what harm could it do?

Now *she* was being ridiculous. There was nothing to gain from letting him back into her life. He'd made his point of view perfectly clear.

But she knew she couldn't resist him, she knew she would give in.

One person, he'd said.

She knew he was right.

At the moment she only needed one person and he was sitting right in front of her.

Some would say she was young and foolish, naïve even, and they might be right, but she was also in love. She desperately wanted a second chance.

She ran her fingers down his arm, entwining their hands together. 'Let's talk about this upstairs,' she said as she stood, pulling him to his feet beside her. In the background she could hear Ruby singing, accompanied by Tilly on her guitar. She ignored all of that and she ignored the throbbing of her injured finger as she led James out of the kitchen and up the stairs. She ignored her conscience, which was asking if she'd given up her argument about Harry. She'd worry about him later. Right now the rest of the world and its problems could wait. With James beside her it was possible to ignore the outside world completely and she wasn't passing up this opportunity.

For the next month Ellie decided to take James's advice that sometimes one person was enough. She concentrated on him and ignored the fact that he was still reluctant to acknowledge his half-brothers. She still hoped he'd come around to the idea of meeting them but for now she kept quiet, choosing not to force the issue in exchange for spending more time with James.

One benefit of their debate over family was that she got to know James's mother and sister. By Ellie's judgement his mother was a confident, intelligent woman who had raised two caring and considerate adults. Because of James's attitude towards marriage Ellie had expected his mother to be scarred by her divorce but it was quite the opposite. He'd been brought up surrounded by strong women and Ellie realised his anti-marriage stance was really about his belief that people couldn't be relied on to make such a commitment. He had a good relationship with his mother and his older sister, Libby, and there was no doubt that his family was an important part of his life. He clearly loved his mum and his sister, as they loved him. He treated them with respect. He was protective and chivalrous without being condescending and he treated her the same way, making her feel safe and adored. It was a good feeling and he was a good man.

But today had been a difficult day. Not un-pleasant, she'd spent it with James and his nieces and nephew at the beach, but she was feeling torn, knowing she should have been elsewhere. She'd enjoyed the afternoon and she had sun-burnt shoulders to prove it. The only thing that had spoiled it was her own guilt.

They had swum, built sandcastles and played beach cricket. James's cricket was good, of course, but she'd been hopeless. Distracted by the picture of James in his board shorts and bare chest, she'd kept missing the ball. Even now, as she sat on the edge of her bed and tried to concentrate on rubbing moisturiser into her sunburnt shoulders, the sight of a semi-naked, still-shirtless James lying beside her was distracting.

But she was still feeling guilty. She'd always spent this day in Goulburn. For the last twelve years that's where she'd been, but today she'd changed her routine, she'd done what she'd wanted to do and now she was feeling guilty.

'Here, let me do that,' James said, reaching for the bottle of lotion. He took over the ministrations. 'Did you have a good afternoon?' he asked.

Her afternoon had been better than good, it had been almost perfect. She didn't regret choosing to spend it with him but she was starting to worry that she would regret some other sacrifices later on, for instance, sacrificing her dreams of having her own family in favour of James. He had almost convinced her that she only needed one person.

Yes, the afternoon had been wonderful but it came at a cost.

'It was almost perfect.'

'Almost?'

'I'm feeling guilty.'

'Guilty? About what?'

'Today is the anniversary of my parents' death. I should have been visiting their graves but instead I was at the beach with you.'

James stopped rubbing the moisturiser into her skin, pausing in mid-circle. 'Why didn't you say something to me earlier? I would have taken you to them.'

'To Goulburn?'

'Why not? Do you want to go now?' he asked, as if it made perfect sense.

Goulburn was more than two hours from Sydney. A round trip would take nearly five hours.

She shook her head. 'Thanks, I appreciate your offer but it's already nearly six o'clock. After an afternoon in the sun I don't think we should tackle that drive.'

He kissed her shoulder. 'I'll take you another day, then. I'll make it up to you.'

'You don't need to do that. It was my decision, my choice. I love spending time with you and your nieces and nephews but today just reminded me of what's missing in my life.'

'What do you mean?'

Could she tell him how she felt? He looked so good lying on her bed, like he belonged there, and she liked the idea of him being there into the future, but her idea of the future might differ from his.

There was no 'might' about it. She knew they had differing views on that topic but it was time for her to be honest with him about some things.

'Do you remember telling me that sometimes one person is enough? That one person is all you need to feel complete?'

He nodded.

'I let myself believe you because I wanted to keep you in my life. You make me feel special and happy and positive but today I missed my family. I want what Libby has.'

'What's that?'

'Kids. A husband. A family of my own. I want to belong to someone who loves me, I want to be someone's wife but I want to be a mother even more.'

James had stopped nodding. He was frowning instead. She wondered if she should stop now, before it was too late.

'Have you some idea of when you might want to have this family?' he asked.

'I've dreamed of having a family of my own since I was about sixteen. Maybe because I lost my parents when I was so young or maybe because I had no siblings or maybe it's just in my genes, but each year that goes past I worry that my dream may be slipping away.'

'So you're not talking years down the track?'

She shook her head. 'I'd hope not.'

'But you're still young. You've got plenty of time.'

Why did everyone tell her that? One day she'd wake up and find that she was old and alone. She couldn't take that chance. 'It took my parents ten years to fall pregnant with me and I was eventually conceived through IVF. It could be the same for me.' That was her greatest fear—what if she couldn't have children?

'Your biological clock is ticking? Is that what you're telling me?'

Ellie nodded. 'I thought I could try living in the moment, I thought I'd see whether I could ignore that yearning, or even if it would pass, but it hasn't. I want a husband, kids, the happily-ever-after. The fairy-tale.'

James swung his legs over the edge of the bed, sitting up beside her. 'That's why it's called a fairy-tale,' he said. 'For the most part it doesn't exist.'

'What doesn't?'

'The whole happily-ever-after. Especially with marriages. My father is a perfect example of that. People aren't prepared for the commitment of marriage.'

'You're not prepared for that commitment, that's what you're saying, isn't it?' Ellie wondered how much of James's attitude stemmed from his father's three failed marriages. It wasn't a stretch of the imagination to see that he'd certainly been influenced by his family history. As had she.

He nodded. 'I'm not cut out for marriage. I've been honest with you all along about that.'

She couldn't argue with him. He was right.

She'd known since the night in Kings Cross that he didn't plan to get married. He'd come close, something she hadn't known until later, but he obviously had no intention of getting that close again.

It was her turn to be truthful. 'And now I'm being honest with you. And with myself. I want my own family. I want the fairy-tale and I intend to have it.'

'And what is the rest of your plan? Where do you go from here?'

'I guess that depends on you.'

'I'm sorry, Ellie. You know that marriage isn't part of my future plan.' He wasn't telling her anything new but she wished it was different.

'No marriage? No kids?'

'You know it's not something I want. I don't *want* to have people depend on me, not in that sense. You have to admit, my family doesn't have a great track record of sticking things out for the long term.'

'You won't think about it?'

James shook his head. 'I have thought about it. A few months ago it was all I thought about and I made my decision then when I broke off my engagement. But I want you to have your dream. I can't help you but I won't stand in your way.' He kissed her softly on the lips before he got up from her bed. 'Go and find the man who will be the father of your children but make sure he treats you right, make sure he loves you. You deserve to be happy.'

He picked up his T-shirt and his car keys and left the room. Left her.

She could hear his footsteps on the stairs and the sound of the front door opening and closing as he walked away. She lay down on the bed, where he had lain, soaking up his warmth. She buried her face in her pillow and inhaled his scent and felt her heart breaking.

She disagreed with his idea that he wasn't cut out for marriage. She was convinced that if he truly fell in love he'd change his mind.

Maybe that was the problem. He didn't love her.

She felt hollow. He had filled her heart with love and she'd felt complete with him.

Should that have been enough for her? Should *he* have been enough? Should she have settled?

No. She shook her head, talking to herself in her empty room. She needed to belong. Even if he'd been prepared to marry her she suspected that in a few years she'd regret not having a family of her own and end up resenting him even though she'd have known all along his feelings on the subject.

As hard as it seemed now, the best thing in the long term was to let him go. She would find someone who would love her back but now, more than ever, she needed her mum. She needed her mum to sit on her bed and stroke her hair. She needed her to kiss her forehead and tell her everything would be better in the morning, just as she'd done when she was ten years old.

She needed her mum and she needed James and she couldn't have either of them.

CHAPTER ELEVEN

SUNDAY was a dreadful day. The sun was shining but all James could see were dark clouds. His house felt dark and lonely. It was quiet, too quiet. The house felt as though it was mourning Ellie's absence. It needed to hear her laughter. *He* needed to hear her laughter.

Don't be ridiculous, he thought, the house couldn't possibly miss Ellie. But he could feel her absence.

He had drifted around the house all day. He needed to get out of here, away from these four walls and his memories. Everything he looked at reminded him of Ellie and if he closed his eyes he could picture her here. He needed to go for a run or a swim.

He went to change into his running clothes but Ellie's bikini was hanging in the shower and her toothbrush was on the basin. He went back upstairs but there were more reminders there. The photo they'd had taken at the surf-club dinner was on the fridge, held in place by an elephant magnet she'd bought for him. A vase of sunflowers took centre stage on the kitchen bench. Brightly coloured lime cushions were now scattered over the sofa and an old wooden coffee table she'd found at a recent trash and treasure market and had repainted in thick lime, white and latte stripes sat on the rug in front of the television. A bowl on the coffee table was filled with a collection of shells and pebbles that Ellie had collected with his nieces. She'd promised to help them decorate photo frames but, thanks to him, she wouldn't be doing that now. His family had adopted Ellie as one of them. How was he going to explain what had happened? How was he going to explain how it had all gone wrong?

He looked around the room. He didn't notice the missing furniture. He didn't notice the missing dining table or sideboard or pictures. All he noticed was that Ellie was missing.

She'd turned his house into a home again. But she'd wanted a family.

Should a home have a family? Could a house be a home *without* a family?

The two weren't mutually exclusive. One person could have a home, but that thought wasn't terribly convincing. Would it be better if more people lived there? People who loved each other?

The phone rang and he pounced on it.

But it wasn't Ellie. It was the real estate agent.

'Dr Leonardi, just wondering how you're going with plans for selling your house. Are you ready to sign the contract?'

He'd delayed putting his house on the market since Ellie had started to spend time there. With her there the house felt loved. When she was there he didn't notice the lack of furniture. When she was there he didn't feel like selling it. Having his house had given them somewhere of their own. The girls' house at Hill Street was filled with laughter but it was also filled with lots of other people and sometimes James had just wanted to have Ellie to himself. He'd loved being in the sanctuary of his own house with her. He didn't want to share her. And he didn't want to sell the house.

'No, it's not going on the market.' It was a link to Ellie. To their memories.

But what of their future? With Ellie in his life he'd been so positive about his future, about himself and the person he could be. But what now? What did his future hold if it wasn't with Ellie? Could he be the man she wanted? Could he give her the things she desired?

When he'd been engaged before he hadn't been able to imagine the future. He'd known the marriage wouldn't last that long. But with Ellie it was different. He couldn't imagine his future *without* her. Already he missed her. He missed hearing her laughter, he missed the feeling of warmth and sunshine she brought to his life. He missed the way she looked at him as if she couldn't wait to get him into her bed.

He wanted her in his life. He needed her in his life. She was his future.

He loved her.

The realisation struck him with full force.

He loved her.

He wanted her.

He needed her.

He picked up a handful of shells and pebbles from the bowl on the coffee table and let them run through his fingers and fall back into the bowl as he thought about Ellie.

He needed to talk to her. He needed to see her and apologise.

He needed to tell her he loved her.

But he had to do it properly. He'd only get one chance to explain. He would take his time and make sure he did it right.

He pulled his phone out of his pocket. Ellie's roster was on there. He knew she was working a late today, he'd already checked, but he wanted to know her movements for tomorrow.

She was on an early shift.

He knew what to do. He was in Theatre tomorrow but after work he'd pick up some supplies and a bottle of champagne, just in case, and invite Ellie to join him for a beach picnic.

Now he had to work out what he would say.

* * *

He'd been at work for less than twenty minutes but his plan was unravelling fast. He was doing a quick ward round and had expected to see Ellie but apparently she'd called in sick. He tried to reach her in the few minutes he had before his theatre list started but she didn't answer her phone.

Every chance he got between patients he called again. He didn't get an answer.

At the end of his day he went straight to the Hill Street house. He assumed if she wasn't well he'd have to reschedule the beach picnic but he needed to see her. He needed to know she was okay.

But there was no answer at Hill Street either. It was an odd situation—a house of four women and the occasional man and nobody home. If Ellie was sick, why wasn't she home? Where was she?

He ducked across the road to the Stat Bar, thinking someone must be there. Someone would be able to tell him what the hell was going on. But neither Tilly, Ruby, Jess nor Ellie were there.

He went home defeated but not deterred. Ellie was on another early tomorrow, he'd just delay his plans for twenty-four hours.

But the following morning she still wasn't at work. Charlotte, the ward physio, was doing the round with him. He pulled her aside at the end of the round. He needed to know what was going on, he was getting worried. 'Charlotte, do you know where Ellie is?'

'She isn't working today. She's off.'

James frowned. According to his phone she was on an early. Had he entered it incorrectly? 'Is she still sick?'

'No, I think she swapped shifts with Sarah. Why don't you ring her?'

He didn't bother explaining that he'd been trying to do that without success. Maybe he'd got her shifts wrong. At the end of rounds he quickly checked the nurses' roster. It showed the shifts for the next fortnight but Ellie's name had been crossed off. Completely. There was a big, thick, black line through her name. All her shifts had been allocated to other staff.

He was really concerned now. His first thought

was for Rob Coleman. Had Penny Coleman got her way? Had Ellie been transferred to a different ward?

He checked his watch. His outpatient clinic was starting in five minutes. He'd have to solve this puzzle later.

Rob was also running a clinic. James told the receptionist he needed to speak to Rob and asked her to interrupt him the moment he was free.

'Can I have a word?' he asked as he stuck his head into Rob's office. Rob gestured for him to come in and James closed the door behind him. 'Do you know where Ellie is?'

'What do you mean?'

'Her name's been taken off the roster. Did you get her transferred?'

Rob frowned. 'Transferred? To where?' He looked completely confused.

'I don't know, that's what I'm trying to find out.'

'I have no idea what you're talking about. I haven't seen Ellie and I don't know where she is.' He gestured to the pile of notes on his desk. 'If you'll excuse me, I have a long list of patients to see, as I'm sure you do,' he said as he dismissed him.

James left Rob's office, none the wiser. He worked his way through his clinic list but instead of working on his research paper for the afternoon, as he'd planned, he took the rest of the day off. He couldn't concentrate until he'd solved the mystery of Ellie's disappearance. He wouldn't be able to concentrate until he knew she was alright.

The squeaky gate heralded his arrival at the Hill Street house and Tilly answered his knock at the door.

'Ellie isn't here,' she said the moment she saw him waiting there.

'Where is she?'

'Why do you need to know?'

Ellie must have spilled the beans about his reluctance to have a family. He certainly wasn't getting his usual warm welcome but he supposed he deserved nothing less. 'Because I owe her an apology.' *Because I love her.*

'About?'

Tilly was standing in the doorway with her arms crossed in front of her chest. James didn't want to have to explain himself to her, it was Ellie who needed to hear him, but he knew, by the expression on Tilly's face, that he wasn't going to get to Ellie without going through Tilly first. And she wasn't going to cave in without a very good reason.

'I said some things to her I didn't mean. I have things to tell her and I need to do it in person. I need to know where she is.'

'She's gone.'

'Gone?' His heart plummeted in his chest. 'Gone where? Why?'

Tilly shrugged. 'She wanted a break.'

'Please, Tilly,' he begged, 'I need to see her. Do you know where she is?'

'No,' she said with a shake of her head. 'She's taken her car and gone.'

'Car?' James frowned. 'She doesn't have a car.'

'She inherited some money from her grandmother and she used some of that to buy a car.'

'When?' He had no idea about an inheritance

and he wondered how many other things he didn't know about Ellie.

'Yesterday,' Tilly sighed. 'Look, I'll try to get in touch with her and if she wants to see you I'll let you know.' She finally took pity on him.

'Thanks, I'd appreciate it.' He took a pen from his pocket and scribbled his mobile number on an old receipt he pulled out of his wallet. 'Please let me know what she says—even if she doesn't want to see me,' he said as he handed her the paper. He hoped she would pass on the message, he hoped Ellie would see him, but either way there was nothing else he could do here.

As he returned to his car he had a sudden flash of insight as to where Ellie might have gone. Was it worth a gamble?

If Tilly convinced Ellie to see him and his hunch was right, he'd be that much closer to her when the call came. It was less than a three-hour trip, he had time, he had nothing but time, and he had nothing to lose.

He jumped into his Jeep and headed south, convinced Ellie would have gone to Goulburn.

Three hours later he was driving aimlessly

around Goulburn. What the hell was he going to do now? He hadn't expected to get to Goulburn without hearing from Ellie. Did this mean she didn't want to see him? Or hadn't Tilly been able to contact her?

Had he made a mistake? Another one?

He kept driving, willing his phone to ring, willing Ellie to materialise before him. But there was no guarantee she was even in Goulburn. That had been a whim, an impulse, on his part. Perhaps she wasn't anywhere near here. And if she was here he had no idea where to start looking. And he had no idea what car to look for either. He should have asked Tilly for that much information at least before he'd taken off on this crazy wild-goose chase.

Did he expect Ellie to be standing in the middle of the street, waiting for him?

What had made him so certain that this was where he'd find her? He was so tired now he couldn't even remember why he'd jumped to that conclusion.

What would he say to her? *He was sorry.*

He drove past the sign for St Patrick's Catholic Cemetery.

What would he say? *He needed her in his life.*

The Catholic cemetery. He hit the brakes and looked in the mirror at the sign at the cemetery gates. Suddenly everything made sense. Ellie had been taught by the nuns at a Catholic boarding school. She was a Catholic. He'd bet his last dollar her parents were buried here. This was where he'd find her. He turned off the road and drove through the gates. This was where he'd find her. With her family.

What would he say? *He loved her.*

A car passed him as he drove along the road past neatly tended graves. He glanced at the driver, hoping to see a familiar face, looking for Ellie. The driver had grey hair, a dark shirt and an old face. It was a priest behind the wheel.

He drove further, searching the grounds for Ellie's familiar figure. He could see a building at the top of a crest, a chapel of some sort. Perhaps he'd have a better view of the cemetery from up there.

Parked beside the chapel was a bright yellow

Volkswagen beetle. James stopped his Jeep alongside the little convertible. He stepped out of his car. There wasn't another soul in sight. He tried the door handle at the chapel's entrance. It was locked. Had the priest locked it before he'd left? Was the cemetery deserted?

His gaze fell on the yellow Volkswagen. No, someone else was here. He just had to find them.

He walked around the building. The hill sloped gently away from him and he could see rows of headstones stretching into the distance as they guarded the gravesites.

And halfway down the hill sat a girl. She shimmered in the late afternoon sun as the light reflected off her golden hair. His breath caught in his throat. Ellie.

This was his chance. His only chance. He needed to get this right.

He walked down the hill towards her, his steps soft, muffled by the spongy grass. He watched her as he descended the slope. She looked so small and fragile sitting alone surrounded by the vast expanse of the cemetery. Surrounded by the headstones.

He made no sound yet when he was a few paces from her she turned around. He could feel their connection pulling him to her. Could she feel it too? Had she felt him approaching?

'James!'

Her blue eyes were glistening and the tip of her nose was red. She'd been crying.

His heart froze in his chest. She was here, alone and crying. Had he done this to her?

He took the last two steps to her side and squatted beside her. He gathered her in his arms, a reflex action, to provide comfort. As his arms encircled her he realised what he was doing and he tensed, hoping she wouldn't push him away. She didn't. She sank into his embrace.

He relaxed and hugged her tight. 'Ellie, my darling, what's wrong?'

She didn't answer but he thought he knew. She would be remembering her family, feeling their loss, feeling alone.

'It's going to be all right,' he whispered. 'I'm here, I've got you.' He was going to make sure she never felt alone again.

Her face was nestled into his shoulder and her

voice was muffled when she asked. 'How did you find me?'

He smiled. 'Goulburn just felt right. I think I'm beginning to understand you but it took me a bit of time to track you down once I got to town. Is it okay that I'm here?'

She nodded. 'But why are you here?'

James changed position, unable to sustain the squat any longer. He sat on the grass behind Ellie and pulled her between his legs so her back was resting against his chest. 'Have you spoken to Tilly?'

'No.' She shook her head and her hair tickled his chin. 'My phone is switched off.'

Why was he here? Having her in his arms again had made him lose track of his thoughts.

What had he wanted to say? *I'm sorry. I need you. I love you.*

'I came to apologise. Seeing my father again brought back all the old feelings of betrayal and loss and fear of commitment. I got so caught up in the past that I let it interfere with us, with our future. You told me that my father's behaviour isn't my responsibility or burden but I've carried it with me for such a long time and it's still influencing my reactions. I was so angry at my father. I thought I'd gotten past all that but obviously I hadn't and I took it out on you. I didn't realise what I'd found in you until you'd gone and when I went looking for you you'd disappeared. You have to come back with me, Ellie, I need you.'

'I'm not sure I can go back.'

What? She had to come back with him. Where else would she go? What else would she do?

'I need a break,' she said. 'It was a mistake to get involved with you. I should have stuck to my rule about no doctors. I need to be away from the ortho ward for a while. I need some space.'

A mistake! No, this wasn't how it was supposed to be. She was supposed to want him as much as he wanted her. He needed her. He loved her.

He changed position again, moving around to kneel in front of her. He took her hands in his and begged her to talk to him. 'Tell me what's wrong. Tell me what I can do to fix this.'

'I don't know if you *can* fix this. We want different things. I'm here trying to sort out what

I want. This is about me and what I need. And I need someone who wants the same things as me. This is about me and you but I'm not sure there can be an "us".'

'What do you mean?'

'I thought what we shared was enough for me. You made me feel special and safe and I thought that was sufficient. It didn't matter that we didn't want the same things. It didn't matter that you didn't want to get married or have children. It wasn't supposed to matter because what we had was only supposed to be temporary. But it does matter. It matters to me because I've fallen in love with you.'

'You love me?'

She nodded and his heart lightened with each movement of her head.

'But I wasn't meant to fall in love,' she said. 'You were supposed to be a distraction but somewhere, somehow, you've gotten inside my heart. You told me that sometimes one person is enough and I wished that were true for me. I wanted it to be true but it's not. I love you but I still need more. I wish that loving you was enough but all I see now are the things I won't have with you. I want a family with you but I can't have that. That's why I needed to get away. It was a mistake and I have to get over you. I will get over you.'

How could she think loving him was a mistake? Her words repeated in his head. Ellie wanted a family and he was here to offer her that. She stood up but he held onto her hand, he wasn't letting her go.

'No, don't.' He stood too and moved downhill so he could look her in the eye. 'This is not a mistake, we are not a mistake. I wanted to be the person you could rely on, the person who would support you and instead I let you down. My history, my past and my stubbornness stopped me from seeing what was important. I haven't been the man I wanted to be for you but I want to change that. I want to give you what you need. I *want* to share my life with you. I want to be yours. That's why I'm here. I want to be your family. My mum, Libby, even Harry if you want, we can all be your family.'

'Harry?'

'You were right about him too,' he admitted. 'None of this is his fault. I'm willing to meet Harry. I'll do it for you.'

'Don't do it for me. Do it because *you* want to.'

'No,' he said with a shake of his head. 'I will do it for you because I love you. I need you in my life and if you want me to get to know my brothers, I will. Please listen to me. This connection we have is a once-in-a-lifetime thing. You feel it too, don't you?' He searched her eyes, looking for confirmation, even though he knew what he said was true. 'I love you and I want you to have a family. I want *us* to be a family.'

He loved her? How she wished that was enough. How she wished it were that easy. She could feel James's heart beating as though it were her own. She could feel every breath he took as though it were her lungs breathing for them both. He was right, they were connected and her body responded to him in a way she'd never responded to anyone before. And she knew she would never love like this again. But it wasn't enough.

'A family means children. To me anyway.' She

had to make it clear. She had to be sure he understood. 'I thought I could have a new dream but I can't. I need children.'

'I want you to have that. I want us to have that.'

He was holding onto her upper arms and his hands were warm and strong, making her feel safe and secure. She hoped this feeling wasn't just an illusion. 'You want children?' He nodded and she frowned. 'What made you change your mind?'

'You,' he said simply. 'Do you remember the photo of us that was taken at the ward dinner? It's on the fridge surrounded by all the paintings Libby's children have done for us? I was looking at those paintings and thinking, What if the pictures had been done by our children? And suddenly I could picture our future. I want a whole lot of blond-haired, blue-eyed children that look like their mother. I want to have a family with you.' He saw her smiling. 'What's so funny?'

'In my mind the children have curly, dark hair with eyes the colour of chocolate, just like their father.'

'Let's agree to have a mixture. As long as we have—'

'Four,' they said together.

'Definitely four,' he repeated. 'I want it all.'

'All?' Could she dare to hope that her dreams could come true?

He nodded. 'But only if I can have it with you. You make my life better. You make me a better person too. You make me think I can be the sort of man you want. The sort of man you deserve. You make me want to try. I want to be the best man I can be and I can only be that if you are in my life. I want to grow old with you. I want to build a life with you. We belong together. I want to watch our children grow, I want to watch our grandchildren grow. I want you to be able to depend on me and I won't let you down. I want you to marry me.'

'What?' Had she heard him right? 'You want to get married?'

'I want you to be the mother of my children but first you need to be my wife.'

'You want to marry *me*?'

'Yes. I'm not letting you go again. Ever.'

'I thought you didn't believe in people's ability to commit?'

'I know I said I wasn't going to get married but I never thought about the implications of that statement until I met you. Until I fell in love with you. When I was engaged before I could never imagine past the wedding, I'd barely been able to imagine that, and I certainly hadn't been able to imagine a long-term future. I'd known I would end up divorced, I thought it was because of my father, that I had too much of my father in me, but now I realise I had the wrong partner. *You* are the one I'm meant to be with and I can't imagine my future without you in it. I get it now. I can see how people believe and trust and hope that their love will last, that their marriage will be the one that makes it. I've found the person I want to spend the rest of my life with and I know we will make it. Together we can do this. I want to share the rest of my life with you. You can depend on me. I promise you that. You are my future.' He knelt on one knee and grinned at her, his chocolate eyes gleamed and her heart swelled with love. 'Now, do you have any more questions or are you going to let me propose properly?'

He really was serious. 'You're going to propose here?'

'I admit this isn't quite what I'd planned. We were supposed to be on the beach last night as the sun set, drinking champagne and toasting our future life together.'

'Last night?'

'I've been looking for you for two days,' he explained. He looked around. They were surrounded by lawns, rose bushes, headstones and silence. 'But it's quite beautiful here too and we are alone, with your family.'

She smiled, touched by his sentiment. 'You're right, this is perfect.'

He nodded and took her hand. Her heart was racing.

'Ellie, my love, I can't imagine my life without you. You bring the sunshine into my world, you bring balance and meaning, you are my centre. I love you, Ellie. Please, will you marry me?'

Tears, happy, emotional tears, were welling in her eyes and her heart was full. That empty spot wasn't empty any more. This was really happening.

She knelt down on the grass before him. 'Everything feels better when you are around,' she told him. 'I feel safe, content, loved and hopeful. Together we can have the life I've dreamed of. I love you.' She kissed him softly on the lips and warmth flooded through her. She loved him and he loved her. He wanted her and she belonged to him. 'And…' she kissed him again '…I will marry you.'

She was loved and she loved in return. She was going to marry the man she adored and have dark-haired babies with blue eyes who smelt like limes or maybe fair-haired babies with chocolate eyes who smelt like sunshine. Any combination was fine with her.

She hugged James to her. He was the love of her life. Her heart was full and her world was perfect.

* * * * *

Mills & Boon® Large Print Medical

May

THE CHILD WHO RESCUED CHRISTMAS	Jessica Matthews
FIREFIGHTER WITH A FROZEN HEART	Dianne Drake
MISTLETOE, MIDWIFE...MIRACLE BABY	Anne Fraser
HOW TO SAVE A MARRIAGE IN A MILLION	Leonie Knight
SWALLOWBROOK'S WINTER BRIDE	Abigail Gordon
DYNAMITE DOC OR CHRISTMAS DAD?	Marion Lennox

June

NEW DOC IN TOWN	Meredith Webber
ORPHAN UNDER THE CHRISTMAS TREE	Meredith Webber
THE NIGHT BEFORE CHRISTMAS	Alison Roberts
ONCE A GOOD GIRL...	Wendy S. Marcus
SURGEON IN A WEDDING DRESS	Sue MacKay
THE BOY WHO MADE THEM LOVE AGAIN	Scarlet Wilson

July

THE BOSS SHE CAN'T RESIST	Lucy Clark
HEART SURGEON, HERO...HUSBAND?	Susan Carlisle
DR LANGLEY: PROTECTOR OR PLAYBOY?	Joanna Neil
DAREDEVIL AND DR KATE	Leah Martyn
SPRING PROPOSAL IN SWALLOWBROOK	Abigail Gordon
DOCTOR'S GUIDE TO DATING IN THE JUNGLE	Tina Beckett

Mills & Boon® Large Print Medical

August

SYDNEY HARBOUR HOSPITAL: LILY'S SCANDAL	Marion Lennox
SYDNEY HARBOUR HOSPITAL: ZOE'S BABY	Alison Roberts
GINA'S LITTLE SECRET	Jennifer Taylor
TAMING THE LONE DOC'S HEART	Lucy Clark
THE RUNAWAY NURSE	Dianne Drake
THE BABY WHO SAVED DR CYNICAL	Connie Cox

September

FALLING FOR THE SHEIKH SHE SHOULDN'T	Fiona McArthur
DR CINDERELLA'S MIDNIGHT FLING	Kate Hardy
BROUGHT TOGETHER BY BABY	Margaret McDonagh
ONE MONTH TO BECOME A MUM	Louisa George
SYDNEY HARBOUR HOSPITAL: LUCA'S BAD GIRL	Amy Andrews
THE FIREBRAND WHO UNLOCKED HIS HEART	Anne Fraser

October

GEORGIE'S BIG GREEK WEDDING?	Emily Forbes
THE NURSE'S NOT-SO-SECRET SCANDAL	Wendy S. Marcus
DR RIGHT ALL ALONG	Joanna Neil
SUMMER WITH A FRENCH SURGEON	Margaret Barker
SYDNEY HARBOUR HOSPITAL: TOM'S REDEMPTION	
	Fiona Lowe
DOCTOR ON HER DOORSTEP	Annie Claydon

0412 LP 2P P2 Medic